Reed felt that punch again.

The one he darn sure shouldn't be feeling right about now.

Not with them so close and her mouth just a few inches from his.

A part of him—definitely not his brain—reminded him that a kiss wouldn't be such a bad thing right now. Their nerves were raw and frayed. Emotions, sky-high. And a kiss might be the ticket to settling them both down.

It was a bad lie, of course.

But the majority of Reed's body just went along with it, and he lowered his head and kissed Addison.

If he thought he'd gotten an avalanche of memories before, that was nothing compared to what he got now. This wasn't one of those little pecks of reassurance. The heat went bone-deep, and it silenced any part of him that was trying to stay logical and keep away from her.

There was nothing logical about this.

REINING IN JUSTICE

USA TODAY **Bestselling Author**

DELORES FOSSEN

ISBN-13: 978-0-373-69824-0

Reining in Justice

This edition published by arrangement with Harlequin Books S.A.

For questions and comments about the quality of this book, please contact us at CustomerService@Harlequin.com.

Printed in U.S.A.

Delores Fossen, a *USA TODAY* bestselling author, has sold over fifty novels with millions of copies of her books in print worldwide. She's received the Booksellers' Best Award and the RT Reviewers' Choice Award, and was a finalist for a prestigious RITA® Award. You can contact the author through her webpage at dfossen.net.

Books by Delores Fossen

HARLEQUIN INTRIGUE

Sweetwater Ranch Series

Maverick Sheriff
Cowboy Behind the Badge
Rustling Up Trouble
Kidnapping in Kendall County
The Deputy's Redemption
Reining in Justice

The Lawmen of Silver Creek Ranch Series

Grayson
Dade
Nate
Kade
Gage
Mason
Josh
Sawyer

Visit the Author Profile page at Harlequin.com for more titles

CAST OF CHARACTERS

Deputy Reed Caldwell—A small-town lawman whose marriage ended over a year ago, but now he's forced to protect his ex-wife and her newborn from a team of vicious kidnappers.

Addison Caldwell—Obsessed with becoming a mother, she turned to a surrogate to get the baby she's always wanted, but in doing so, she also kept secrets from Reed.

Emily Caldwell—The newborn who's the target of the kidnappers. But why?

Dominic Harrelson—Addison's attorney who might have cut corners for her. Or for himself.

Blake Rooney—A PI that Addison hired to find the truth about baby Emily, but he might not be the person he seems.

Gunther Quarles—A rich and powerful judge who could be connected to some illegal adoptions and surrogacies.

Chapter One

There was blood on the porch.

That kicked up Deputy Reed Caldwell's pulse a significant notch. He'd already drawn his Colt .45, but he called for backup because this wasn't looking good.

He walked to the end of the porch, his breath mixing with the early morning air and causing a filmy haze around him. Reed peered into the window of the dining room and saw that the table and chairs had been toppled over. There'd been some kind of struggle.

Mercy. What was going on?

No sign of any intruders or the owner—his ex-wife, Addison.

But Reed was pretty sure she was inside somewhere. Alive. Or at least she had been a few minutes earlier when she'd made a frantic nine-one-one call to the Sweetwater Springs Sheriff's Office. Reed had intercepted the call because he'd been on his way home after pulling a night shift and was driving right by her place.

"Someone's trying to break in."

That was the only thing Addison had managed to say before the line went dead. There was no bad weather to cause a dead phone line. No maintenance that he'd heard about. Just the frantic one-line message.

Reed hadn't been sure what to expect when he arrived at the small country house Addison had recently inherited, but he'd parked by her mailbox, twenty yards or so from the house so that the sound of his truck engine wouldn't alert anyone. Even with the extra precaution, Reed had figured this would turn out to be a false alarm. Or else he'd find Addison cowering inside while some would-be burglars were making their escape.

But he definitely hadn't expected blood. Or the toppled furniture.

Maneuvering around the drops of blood, he turned the doorknob. It was unlocked. And he eased open the front door. Reed wasn't a blood expert, but there were more drops in the foyer, and it looked like high-velocity spatter as if someone had been hit hard.

It didn't take him long to see that more stuff had been knocked down in the entry. A small table. The landline phone that'd been ripped from the wall.

Most noticeable, though—an empty infant car seat.

Since Addison had recently adopted a baby, the seat wasn't unexpected, but it put a knot in Reed's gut to see it tossed on its side like that.

Where was the baby?

And where the heck was Addison?

If it was her blood, then she'd clearly been hurt. Maybe hurt badly enough that she couldn't even call out to him.

That didn't help the knot in his stomach.

His backup wouldn't be there for at least fifteen minutes, but Reed didn't want to waste any more time in case she was bleeding out. Listening, he quietly stepped inside, pivoted, checking every visible corner of the house. No one was in his line of sight, but he heard some movement in the adjacent living room. He peered around the edge of the wall, and his heart walloped against his chest.

Addison.

There was blood on her forehead and smeared in the side of her light brown hair. Her eyes were wide, and there was a large swatch of silver duct tape covering her mouth. The same tape had been used to tie her hands and feet, but despite the restraints, she was frantically trying to crawl toward him.

Still keeping watch around them, Reed hurried to her and eased back the tape from her mouth.

"They're upstairs," she whispered, the words rushing out with her breath. She tried to crawl again while fighting to get her hands and ankles free.

"Who's up there?" Reed asked, looking in that direction.

"I think they're kidnappers."

Hell. Sweetwater Springs wasn't a perfect town, but he hadn't expected kidnappers to break into someone's house.

"Get me out of this," Addison insisted, still fighting the tape.

Reed pulled out his pocketknife, sliced through the layers, but the moment that Addison was free, she sprang to her feet. Or rather she tried. She stumbled and probably would have fallen if Reed hadn't caught onto her. She smacked right against him and into his arms.

Despite the nightmare of the moment, that gave him a jolt of memories. Of when they'd been married and she'd been in his arms for a totally different reason. However, Reed shoved those memories aside and instead focused on trying to hold back an injured woman who was hell-bent on barreling up the stairs where she could be killed.

Reed took her by the shoulder and forced eye contact. *How many are up there?* he mouthed.

She shook her head. "Two, maybe three." Her breath broke. "I saw them on the porch, then called for help, but one of them hit me."

That explained the blood. But not why they'd broken in.

"I heard them say something about the baby," she added in a hoarse whisper. "Emily's upstairs sleeping."

Reed figured that was her adopted baby's name. And if there were indeed two to three kidnappers trying to take the child, then he needed to get to the baby now. The only problem was, he didn't hear any movement upstairs, and he hadn't seen any extra vehicles when he'd driven up.

Of course, this could be just a simple burglary, and the men could have mentioned the baby to threaten Addison, to make sure she cooperated and didn't fight back.

Addison wasn't rich, but the house she'd inherited from her aunt might have something burglars would want, and it was off the beaten path. The men might be looking for quick cash or jewelry. Or maybe they didn't even know that anyone would be there because the place had been empty for months. Addison had returned only a few days earlier.

Or so Reed had heard from the gossip mill.

After their bitter split, Reed had done his best to avoid any and all info and gossip about his ex.

He fired off a text to his backup and fellow deputy, Colt McKinnon, who would no doubt be arriving soon. Reed didn't want Colt walking in on this without some kind of heads-up.

"Stay here," Reed warned Addison when he finished the text.

She didn't, of course. Even on good days Addison could be hardheaded, but he doubted anything short of duct-taping her again would get her to stop. Not with her baby in possible danger.

"At least stay quiet and behind me," Reed amended.

This time she listened, but she grabbed an umbrella from a basket next to the overturned table. She was still shaky, her breathing was way too fast, but she kept up with him as he eased up the stairs. Reed had made it just a few steps from the top when the sounds stopped him cold.

Footsteps and whispers.

"They're in my aunt's old bedroom," she muttered. "I'm using it as a temporary office."

Better there than the nursery, but that didn't make things safer. Burglars could still do all sorts of bodily harm—Addison's head was proof of that—but maybe they'd leave the baby out of this.

Reed eased onto the stairwell but had to take hold of Addison when she tried to dart past him. She didn't try to go toward the sounds in her office but rather to the room at the end of the hall.

The nursery, no doubt.

There wasn't anyone moving around in there, not that Reed could hear anyway. The only movement was coming from the room on his right.

He shot Addison a warning glance for her to stay put, and he hoped this time she'd listen. Thankfully, she did. With a death grip on the umbrella, she waited and held her breath.

Reed was holding his breath, too, when he glanced around the edge of the door of her office. Like in the downstairs, things had been tossed and turned in here, too. There were two men dressed all in black, their backs to him, and they were stuffing papers and a laptop into a large satchel.

Both were armed.

"We got two minutes," one of the men called out. "Don't want the locals in here on this."

Locals. As in Reed or someone else from the Sweetwater Springs Sheriff's Office. Did the men know Addison had managed to call him? If so, they probably thought the cops were still en route. They likely wouldn't have known that Reed would be driving right by her place at the exact moment she'd needed him.

Reed glanced back at Addison to make sure she was okay. She hadn't stayed put for long and was now inching her way to the nursery. That maybe wasn't a bright idea, but Reed had enough to deal with now. Besides, Addison would likely do whatever it took to protect the baby, and that meant he could focus on these morons ransacking the place.

"You think we got it all?" one of the men asked his partner.

"Can't be sure," he answered. "Let's go to plan B and torch the place."

Reed didn't have time to curse or try to get Addison and the baby out of there. He heard a vehicle approaching. Colt, no doubt. The siren was off, but it still must have alerted one of the men, because he pivoted, his attention zooming right to Reed.

"I'm Deputy Reed Caldwell," he identified himself.

Both men raised their guns. Not ordinary weapons but ones rigged with silencers. One of them fired, just as Reed scrambled to the side, and even though it wasn't a normal loud blast, the bullet tore through the doorjamb.

Hell's bells.

He hadn't wanted to get into a gunfight with anyone but especially not without backup in place.

Another shot quickly came at him, and Reed hurried out of the way while he readied himself to return fire. He latched on to Addison and pulled her into the adjacent open doorway. It was her old bedroom, still decorated as it'd been when she was in high school.

"The bullets could hit Emily," she said, fighting to get away from him. But she didn't go toward the nursery. She hurried to her nightstand and took out a gun. That definitely hadn't been there when she was in high school.

"Reed?" someone yelled. It was Colt, and it sounded as if he was already inside the house.

"Upstairs." Even though the men had fired guns rigged with silencers, Reed figured Colt had heard the shots and knew that this situation had gone from bad to worse.

However, *worse* took yet another bad turn.

No more shots, but it was a sound that got Addison moving fast.

Soft cries.

Definitely the baby, especially since the cries were coming from the nursery. Reed had to put Addison in a body lock to keep her from racing out into the hall where those men could kill her with an easy shot.

"Let's get the hell out of here now," he heard one of the men growl.

Reed didn't want them to escape, but he also didn't want any more shots fired in the vicinity of the baby. He pulled Addison to the side of the bed so he'd be in a better position to protect them both, and he braced himself for the men to come running past them. If that happened, he could stop them before they got to the nursery.

Maybe.

"Watch out, Colt!" Reed shouted down. Because he figured these guys might eventually head Colt's way if they didn't go to the nursery. If they did indeed run for the stairs, then Reed could let go of Addison and race after them.

But no one came out of the makeshift office.

Reed still heard the scrambling around. Still heard voices. However, the men didn't come his way or toward the stairs.

The seconds crawled by. With his heartbeat crashing in his ears. His hand tight and hard on his gun. Addison struggling to get loose. The baby's cries.

"They're getting away," Colt called out.

Reed had no choice but to let go of Addison, and he hurried to the doorway so he could glance into her office.

No men.

But the window was wide-open. He hadn't spotted a ladder when he drove up, but they'd obviously gotten out somehow.

"They're on foot," Colt added, "and I'm in pursuit."

Reed raced to the office window and looked down. Not the best idea he'd ever had. The two men were there on the ground. A ladder, too. Not the standard metal one but the portable rope kind that could be carried in an equipment bag.

One of them turned and fired a shot directly at Reed. The bullet tore through the window and sent a spray of glass over the room. He felt the sting of a cut near his eyes, ignored it and took aim.

Reed fired.

His shot slammed into the nearest man's shoulder, and even though the guy stumbled, his partner took hold of him, and they ran toward the barn. Reed got a glimpse of the black SUV parked inside, and both men barreled into the vehicle. The SUV was out of his firing range, but if the driver came back toward the road, he might get another shot at stopping them.

But then Reed saw something else.

A second rope ladder.

This one was three windows over, and it took him a moment to realize it was outside the nursery. That had barely registered when he heard the scream.

Addison.

Reed bolted out of the office, directly toward her scream, and he found her in the nursery. She was at the open window, climbing out on the rope ladder.

The crib was empty.

"They have her," Addison sobbed. "They took Emily."

Reed pulled her back so he could get a better look at the SUV as it sped out from the barn. The windows were heavily tinted, too dark for him to see inside. But he did spot Colt.

"Aim for the tires," Reed shouted down to his fellow deputy.

If the baby was indeed inside the vehicle, he didn't want to risk a stray bullet going her way.

Colt took aim. Fired. But the shot smacked off the bumper.

"Go after them!" Addison begged.

He did. He barreled down the stairs and toward the door. But he was already too late.

Reed barely managed to ready his gun before the SUV sped away.

Chapter Two

Everything inside Addison was spinning out of control. She wanted to keep screaming, to force those men to bring back Emily, but more than that, she just wanted to stop the SUV and put an end to this nightmare.

"Give me back my baby!" Addison yelled, but she had no idea if they could even hear her.

She was still dizzy, her head was pounding, but she took hold of the railing as she ran down the steps. Reed was right there at the bottom to catch her again, but she didn't want him to hold her back. Addison darted onto the porch, looking for any sign of Emily or those men.

And her heart dropped to her knees.

There was the wall of dust that the tires had kicked up as the SUV sped out of her driveway.

They'd gotten away.

God, no.

This couldn't be happening.

"No license plates," Colt shouted out to them, "but I'm calling in a description of the vehicle."

Maybe that meant every cop in the area would respond so they could stop the kidnappers, but Addison couldn't just stand by and wait for it to happen. She had to do something. *Anything.* Even if it meant risking her life.

Even if it meant risking Reed's and Colt's.

The only thing that mattered now was saving Emily.

"We have to go after them," she told Reed. She was willing to beg if necessary. One way or another, she was leaving to follow the SUV.

Reed glanced at her, as if trying to decide what to do, and then ran toward his truck by the mailbox that the SUV had skirted around. He jumped inside.

"You need to stay here with Colt," he grumbled to her.

But again, he didn't stop her when she threw open the passenger door and dropped down onto the seat beside him. Addison still had her gun, and even though she wasn't sure she could see straight enough to aim, she'd do whatever it took to get her baby back.

The memory of Emily's cries echoed through her head, but she tried to shut them out. Tried to hold herself together. Hard to do with everything crashing down on her.

"I can't lose her," she heard herself say.

She also heard the hoarse sob that followed. And worse, felt the tears burn her eyes. Addison couldn't stop them, but tears and sobs wouldn't help now. Her little girl needed her to stay strong.

"You won't lose her," Reed promised.

Of course, it was a promise he couldn't really give her, but Addison didn't care. She would take anything she could get right now. She only wanted them to catch up with the SUV so she could have Emily back in her arms where she belonged. Too bad she didn't know how to do that, but she was certain if she could just see Emily, she'd figure out a way.

"Put on your seat belt," Reed reminded her as he sped away from her house.

Somehow, despite her shaking hands, Addison managed to get the seat belt on, and she grabbed on to the dash when Reed peeled out onto the road. To the left was a dead end. The main road was to the right, and that was the way he went. It was almost certainly the path the SUV had taken, too, and she prayed the kidnappers stayed on the road so that Reed and she could find them.

"I don't see them," Addison said, and she cursed the sharp curves in this part of the road.

There were too many blind spots. Plus, there were old ranch trails that a vehicle could pull into and hide on. Reed and she couldn't lose them, and heaven knew where they'd take Emily. She might never see her baby again, and that felt like a crushing vise around her heart.

"Who are these men?" Reed asked.

She had to shake her head. "I don't know."

And she didn't. Addison had gotten glimpses of their faces, and she was certain she'd never seen them before.

"Think," Reed insisted. "Tell me everything you remember about what happened."

Not easy to remember anything with her thoughts flying around like an F-5 tornado, but Addison drew in several hard breaths, forced herself to clear her head as much as she could.

"I came down to get a cup of coffee, and I saw them on the porch. There were two of them, but I think there was another one. I got a glimpse of something or someone behind me before I was bashed on the head."

Reed said something she didn't catch. "There must have been a third one. I saw two men running from your office window. The third must have taken the baby while the other two were rummaging around in there."

Just the thought of it tore her into a million little pieces.

Some stranger grabbing her baby while she was

taped up downstairs. Addison couldn't bear it if they hurt her.

But who would hurt a precious little baby?

Emily was only two months old. No one could possibly want to do anything bad to someone so young and innocent. Did that mean this was some kind of kidnapping for ransom? If so, she didn't have much, but she'd give them everything she had, everything she could get her hands on.

"What do you think they wanted?" Reed asked.

Addison was about to go with the ransom idea, but then she froze, the thought flashing through her mind. It couldn't be *that.*

Could it?

"What?" Reed pressed when she didn't answer.

It took her a moment to get it out. "I hired a P.I. to make sure everything was okay with the...adoption."

Reed glanced at her, and even though she hadn't thought it possible, there was even more concern on his face. Probably because there'd been a lot in the news lately about a black-market baby ring that'd been uncovered in the area.

"I didn't do anything illegal to get Emily," Addison quickly added. "But..."

And that was when her explanation ground to a halt.

How much should she tell him?

Not the whole truth, that was for sure. Not now anyway with everything else going on. Maybe not ever.

"You trust this P.I. you hired?" Reed asked. He didn't slow down. Didn't glance at her again. He just kept driving at breakneck speed around the curvy road.

"I thought I did. He had excellent references, and he contacted me to say he'd been doing other background checks for families with recently adopted babies. The P.I.'s name is Blake Rooney."

And once she had her baby safely back in her arms, then she'd make sure Rooney hadn't had any part of this.

Whatever *this* was.

If the P.I. had done something wrong, then Addison would make sure he paid, and paid hard. But for now, she had to battle herself. The tears came again. The fear, too. It felt as if it were choking the life right out of her.

"Focus," Reed insisted. Probably because he sensed that she was about to lose it. "Did this P.I. find out anything suspicious about the adoption?"

It took her a moment to get her mouth working. "I don't think so. He was supposed to email me a report this morning."

Reed cursed. "Those men were going through papers in your office. And they took your laptop. They were clearly looking for something."

Oh, God. Had it been the P.I.'s report they were after?

If so, Addison wasn't even sure she'd received it yet. She had planned to check her email after she'd had coffee if Emily hadn't wakened yet. However, she hadn't gotten the chance to do that, because the kidnappers had shown up.

"What exactly was the P.I. looking for?" Reed asked.

Again, she had to fight through the panic so she could answer. Where the heck was that SUV?

"I just asked Rooney to do background checks on the lawyers and the woman who gave birth to Emily," she answered.

And maybe Rooney had found something. But what? What could he have found that would have sent a team of kidnappers after her baby?

"You're bleeding," Reed let her know. And he grabbed a handful of tissues from a box between the seats and pressed it against her head.

She didn't feel the blood. Didn't feel any pain at all and was about to push the tissues away when Reed rounded the next curve.

There. Just ahead.

The SUV.

Not driving away from them.

It had stopped right in the middle of the road.

Reed cursed, slammed on his brakes, and tried to push her down onto the seat. Addison batted him away because there was no chance she would stay out of this. Not after what she saw in front of them.

There was a man dressed all in black holding Emily.

At least she was pretty sure it was her baby. Addison couldn't see any part of the baby's face, but she recognized the blanket. It was the pink one that'd been in Emily's crib.

"Wait!" Reed shouted when Addison bolted from the truck.

She didn't listen. Addison hurried out and faced the man head-on. He had a gun in his right hand, the baby cradled in his left arm, but he didn't take aim at her.

Addison soon realized why.

There were two other gunmen inside the SUV, and both of them had weapons trained on Reed and her. One of them was slumped forward, bleeding, but that might not affect his aim.

Reed got out and pointed his gun at the driver.

"Give me the baby," Addison insisted.

Even though she still had hold of her gun, she also didn't aim it at the men. She didn't want to give them any reason to start shooting again.

Addison glanced around to make sure another vehicle wasn't coming. This wasn't a busy road, but that didn't mean the deputy, Colt, or someone else couldn't come around the corner and crash into them. It was early, and there was still some slick moisture on the road surface. Not the best place for an impromptu meeting, but at least she had her baby in front of her.

"We'll trade the kid for you," the man said, tipping his head to Addison. He was big. Well over six feet tall and had bulky shoulders. It was the same man she'd seen on her porch before she was hit.

"No," Reed answered. "Hand her the baby and drop your weapon. You, too," he added to the others. "I want those guns on the ground now."

Reed sounded like the cowboy cop that he was. A man with a badge and in charge. However, she hadn't expected the kidnappers just to do as he'd ordered.

And they didn't.

The man holding Emily stared at Addison. "You want to save her? Then get in the SUV with us now."

Addison wanted to do just that if it would get Emily safely out of there. But she had just enough sanity left to know this was almost certainly a trick. If she got into the vehicle, there was nothing to stop them from killing Reed and driving away with both Emily and her.

Still, she'd be with her baby.

"Don't," Reed warned her when Addison took a step toward the man.

"It's the only way," the man insisted. "We have to know what you learned and who you told."

That stopped Addison in her tracks, and she shook her head. "I didn't learn anything."

"Time's up," the driver said, ignoring her denial.

He pointed his gun right at her. "We need to get out of here now."

She braced herself for an attack. But it didn't happen. The man holding Emily charged forward, and he thrust the baby toward Reed. Addison got a glimpse of what was inside the blanket then.

Emily!

The relief was instant. *Thank God.* And her baby appeared to be unharmed. She was awake and flailing her arms around as if she was about to start crying.

"Take her!" Addison shouted to Reed.

Reed did. He moved fast, and he scooped the baby from the man's arms. In the same motion, the gunman reached out for Addison, and he probably would have managed to latch on to her arm if the sound hadn't distracted him. The kidnapper glanced up when the vehicle came around the corner.

It was Colt.

The deputy had obviously taken the turn too fast and was in a full skid. His dark blue truck flew past them just as Reed got the baby inside his own vehicle.

Addison ran there, too, racing toward Emily. However, she'd barely made it a step when Colt's truck crashed right into the side of the SUV. The air was suddenly filled with the sounds of metal scraping against metal.

The gunman shouted something but got out of the way in time. He was just a blur of motion from the corner of Addison's eye, and she didn't wait to see where he'd land or what would happen next.

She hurried as fast as she could back toward Reed's truck, jumped inside and scooped the baby up into her arms.

Emily didn't cry. The baby only looked up at Addison as if trying to figure out what was going on.

"Get down!" Reed yelled.

This time, Addison did exactly as he said. She dropped to the floor, sheltering Emily's body with hers.

She heard the squeal of the tires on the asphalt.

Followed by a shot.

Addison looked up in time to see the bashed-in SUV coming right toward them. Obviously the crash hadn't disabled the engine.

There was no time for Reed to get his truck out of the way. He could only brace himself for a collision, and Addison tried to do the same. The SUV was damaged, banged up on the side where Colt's truck had hit it, but that didn't mean it couldn't have a hard enough impact to hurt the baby.

Reed managed to get off a shot to try to stop the driver, but the bullet skipped off the roof of the SUV just as it darted around his truck.

And the kidnappers sped away.

Chapter Three

Reed finished his call with the sheriff and watched as the medic put the bandage on Addison's head. She didn't even react. She had her attention solely on the baby cradled in her arms. The little girl seemed to be sleeping peacefully now, but Emily still occasionally sucked the bottle that the nurse had made for her.

The medic had cleaned away the blood from Addison's forehead, but there was a dark blue bruise already forming. The same color as her troubled eyes.

"Any sign of the kidnappers?" Addison asked the moment Reed put his phone away. She was still ash pale except for that bruise, and along with the relief of being safe at the hospital, he could also see the fear etched on her face.

Reed had to shake his head. "Not yet. But everyone's out looking for them. Plus, there's a CSI team headed out to your place. They might find some prints or DNA to tell us who they were."

After all, Reed had shot one of them, so there'd be blood in the backyard. If the guy was in the system, then they could get a match, and in Reed's experience, once they had a name, they could start figuring out what had gone on. People generally didn't commit assorted felonies, including attempted kidnapping and murder, for no reason.

"Thank you," Addison told Reed when the medic walked away. "You saved our lives."

True, but only because they'd gotten lucky by being in the right place at the right time. Reed hated it'd taken something as fragile as luck to make that happen.

Luck might not be on their side again.

After the SUV sped away, his lawman's instincts had been for him to turn his truck around and go in pursuit, but it would have been too big a risk. Those gunmen could have started shooting again. Reed wanted to catch the dirtbags, but he hadn't wanted to do that by putting Addison, the baby and even Colt in further danger.

Even though the adrenaline was still pumping through him, Reed forced himself to sit down next to Addison in the E.R. examining stall. Over the past year he'd completely avoided any contact with his ex, and she'd done the same with him. But this wasn't personal now.

He repeated that to himself.

Funny, but it always felt personal with Addison, and that wasn't personal in a good way. Too many old, bad memories were in the mix, too.

Before the split, they'd been married for nearly three years, had dated five years before that, but their long relationship had soured big-time when Addison pressed and pressed him to have kids.

And they'd tried despite his reservations about fatherhood and the strain that pregnancy would put on her body.

However, her infertility had only added to their differences. One failed in vitro procedure after another, and they'd finally pulled the plug a year ago on both the baby plans and the marriage, and he had filed for a divorce. Addison had moved to San Antonio, and Reed had thought he might never see her again.

Clearly, he'd been wrong about that, because here she was and apparently in a boatload of trouble.

"I was only going to be here a few weeks," Addison volunteered. "Just enough time to get the place ready to sell. If they'd come after me while I was at my apartment in San Antonio, they might have succeeded in taking her."

It was true, but Reed didn't bother confirming it. Addison was already shaken up enough. "Did the P.I., Blake Rooney, visit you at your apartment?"

She nodded. "He came earlier this week."

Reed didn't like the timing of that. "Did you tell him you were coming to your late aunt's place here in Sweetwater Springs?"

Addison shook her head, at first, but then the alarm went through her eyes. "He saw my suitcases and baby things and asked if I was going on a trip. I told him I'd inherited a house and was going to sell it. You think Rooney had something to do with those kidnappers?"

"Maybe. Colt's trying to contact him now," Reed explained. "We'll make sure he's okay and bring him in for questioning."

It was possible Rooney had indeed suspected something illegal about Emily's adoption or had even been a part of it. That was Reed's top theory now. But it must have been many steps past being bad for someone to send three armed men to steal whatever the P.I. had discovered.

Or to learn what Addison might have done.

If she had indeed participated in an illegal adoption, then someone might have wanted to cover it up.

The problem was she might not even have known she'd done anything illegal. That meant Addison would need to be questioned thoroughly to make sure everything was aboveboard.

The door to the examining room opened, and a nurse stuck her head in. "You'll be able to go soon. Just waiting on the paperwork from the doctor."

Soon couldn't come soon enough for Reed. He needed to put some space between Addison and him, but that wouldn't happen until he started to get some answers to all those questions he had.

"Why'd you decide to go ahead and adopt a baby?" Reed asked, figuring it was a simple enough question and a good way to go back to the beginning. "Being a single parent couldn't have been an easy decision for you."

Something flashed through Addison's eyes. Maybe because this wasn't exactly a safe subject for them. After all, it'd been at the root of their breakup.

"I'm thirty-four and decided not to wait any longer for the right fertility treatment," she finally answered. "Or wait for Mr. Right, for that matter. Haven't had much luck in that department."

She paused just long enough for him to understand he was in the Mr. Wrong category, but Reed hadn't needed the pause to get that.

"You know how much I've always wanted to be a mom," she added a moment later.

He did, and that said it all. Addison had wanted it and had gone for it. But maybe in going for it, she had cut the wrong kinds of corners.

"If you hired Rooney, you must have suspected something wasn't right," Reed tossed out there.

She got that look in her eyes again, as if this was the

last thing on earth she wanted to discuss. Tough. They were discussing it.

"Not suspected. But I was worried," she explained, "because of all the things I was hearing."

Yeah, he got that, too. The black-market baby rings had been all over the news. Pregnant women had been kidnapped and their babies sold. In some cases, the birth mothers had been murdered, but others had escaped. Maybe Addison had wanted to make sure one of those escapees wasn't Emily's real birth mother. If so, that birth mother could step in and take Emily from her long after the adoption had been finalized.

"Could this be related to something…well, personal?" he asked. "Like maybe a boyfriend or ex who wants to get back at you?"

She shook her head, seemingly relieved, and looked away. "You're the only ex I have who hates me."

Reed opened his mouth to say he didn't hate her. That he only hated the demands she'd put on him to become a father.

However, it was best not to go there.

"But, no. There's no recent ex. No recent anything since Emily," Addison said.

Maybe, but Reed kept pressing. "What about your job? Are you still working as an accountant?"

Another nod. "But I'm not working on anything that'd cause kidnappers to come after Emily and me. I'm sure," she added before he could challenge that.

"I'll need a list of all your recent clients anyway," Reed continued. Addison dealt with people's bank accounts and such, and it was possible someone hadn't wanted her to uncover some illegal activity.

"I'll give you whatever you need to find those men," she said, her voice shaky again. Actually, she was shaky, too. The room wasn't cold, but he figured she was about to deal with an adrenaline crash.

A sob tore from her mouth, and she leaned her head against him. Reed would have had to be a coldhearted jerk to push her away. But he made things a lot worse by putting his arm around her and pulling her against him.

"I'm scared," Addison whispered.

She had reason to be scared, but Reed didn't voice that. Nor did he ease her away though the shaking started to ease up a little.

He settled for saying, "I don't think these guys were amateurs. They could have killed you the moment they broke into your house. They didn't. Instead they wanted to know what you'd learned and who you'd told. Maybe about the adoption, maybe about something else. I think that's why they took your files, laptop and cell phone."

"Oh, God." Addison got to her feet so fast that she startled the baby. "Last night I called Jewell at the county jail." She frantically shook her head. "I just wanted to tell her about Emily."

Of course. *Jewell.* Yet another source of bad blood between them.

Jewell McKinnon and Addison were friends despite their age difference, and Jewell was his boss's estranged mother. Estranged in a very bad way because twenty-three years ago, Jewell had abandoned her sons and husband and left town under a cloud of suspicion that she'd murdered her lover. Well, the suspicion had caught up with her, and now Jewell was in jail waiting on her upcoming murder trial.

A trial that would put Addison and Reed at odds yet again since Addison believed Jewell was 100 percent innocent. He thought the woman was as guilty as sin.

Plus, Reed wasn't exactly fond of Jewell abandoning people he cared about—like Jewell's sons.

"Call the county jail," she insisted. "Make sure these men don't go after Jewell."

"The jail's secure," Reed reminded her, and he tried to make her sit back down. "If those men show up there, they'll be caught."

Of course, Reed doubted they'd get that lucky or the men would be that stupid. It was ironic, but right now Jewell was safer than the rest of them.

"I also called my attorney, Dominic Harrelson," Addison quickly added. "You think they'd go after him?"

Reed couldn't rule that out so he made a quick call to the sheriff, Cooper McKinnon, and asked him to have someone check on the attorney. "Who else did you contact?" he pressed when he'd finished the call.

"No one. I've been spending all my time with Emily. I haven't had much time for anything else."

For the investigation, that was a good thing. Fewer contacts meant fewer people might be in danger.

Of course, Reed had no idea how many people were involved in this.

The door opened again, and Reed automatically moved away from Addison so he could stand in front of her. However, it wasn't the kidnappers or the nurse. But rather Colt. And Reed hadn't moved fast enough away from Addison, because Colt had seen the close contact between them.

Colt frowned, added something that Reed didn't need to catch to understand. His fellow deputy certainly knew the emotional wringer Reed had been through with Addison and the divorce. Reed was right there with Colt in the disapproval department, and he made a note to keep his hands off Addison.

Reed soon realized, though, it wasn't just the close-contact stuff that'd put the look on Colt's face. Colt and he had been deputies together for over six years, and that was plenty enough time for Reed to know something was wrong.

"Before the CSI team could get out there and have a look around, someone torched Addison's house," Colt explained. He'd said it practically under his breath, but Addison must have heard it, because she gasped and clutched the baby even closer to her.

"They burned down my aunt's house?" she asked. And even though Reed had told himself that there'd be no more close contact, he took hold of Addison again because she looked ready to sink to the floor.

"They did cleanup, too, of the blood in the yard," Colt added. "Still, they might have left something behind."

Addison was mumbling, shaking her head.

And crying.

Yes, the tears came, too, but Reed tried to focus on what this turn of events meant. The men were pros, definitely. Someone with lots of money and with a whopper of a motive. But what?

Everything that Addison had said and done in the past couple of days could be critical to finding out what they wanted.

And how to stop them.

"I have to get out of here," Addison insisted.

Colt and Reed exchanged glances. "She needs to give us a statement about what happened," Colt reminded him.

Reed hadn't forgotten that, but he also didn't think Addison was in any shape to do it right now. Except he rethought that when he looked at her. She was still pale. Still well past the shaky stage, but she met him eye to eye.

"What can I do to stop them?" she asked.

That was a good question, but it wasn't the foremost one in Reed's mind. "We'll be the ones doing the stopping. You need to be in protective custody."

She blinked. "Yours?"

Reed went through the options. There weren't that many.

Either Addison would have to be with him or she'd have to stay with one of Jewell's sons—sons who disliked Addison because of her friendship with their murdering, abandoning mother. With the trial bearing down on them, that would breach all sorts of legal issues because Addison would no doubt be called as a character witness for Jewell.

"I'll stay with you for now," Reed said. But he'd remedy that soon even if he had to call in the Rangers or the marshals.

"Take her statement, Reed," Colt added over his shoulder as he left.

He intended to do just that, but something wasn't right here. Something he couldn't quite put his finger on. That *something wasn't right* feeling only got worse when Addison dodged his gaze again.

"Who was involved in the adoption?" he asked Addison, and that was when Reed noticed she'd gone pale again.

Hell.

"You did cut corners," he spat out.

She swallowed hard. "Not like you're thinking. I went through a private agency called Dearborn, but they don't only do adoptions." She paused, gathered her breath. "They have surrogates."

"Surrogates," he repeated. Reed gave that a moment to sink in.

It didn't sink in well.

Oh, man.

"I hired a surrogate to carry her," she said. Addison's gaze came to his. "Emily is *our* baby."

Chapter Four

The only thing Addison could do now was wait for the fallout. And there would be fallout. She was certain of it. She'd just delivered a bombshell to Reed. One that was going to make him hate her even more than he already did.

If that was possible.

Reed's gaze rifled from her. To Emily. And back again.

"Oh, man," he said, and Reed just kept repeating it while he got up and went to the other side of the stall. As far away from Addison as he could get.

"I'm sorry," Addison said.

That covered a multitude of things but not Emily herself. Addison wasn't sorry at all that she had her precious little girl, but she'd made mistakes to get the baby.

Well, one big mistake anyway.

Reed groaned, put his hands on the sides of his head and turned away from her. For several long moments he stood there, repeating that "Oh, man" before he swung back around to face her.

"It's true," Reed said. Not a question exactly, but Addison nodded. "How? Why?" he asked.

His questions no doubt covered a multitude of things, too, so Addison started from the beginning. Well, the beginning after the end of their marriage, that is. The past year had been eventful to say the least.

"Six weeks after we separated, I got the divorce papers your lawyer sent. Even though I'd known they were coming, I was still shaken up." A massive understatement, but it wasn't something Reed would want to hear now.

Maybe not ever.

He'd washed his hands of their marriage and wasn't the sort to take treks down memory lane.

"As you know, I'd already had two miscarriages and three failed in vitro procedures, and there was only one of our embryos left in storage," she continued. "I figured I stood a better chance of having it work with a surrogate than me trying again."

His jaw muscles seemed to freeze. Not his eyes, though. He glared at her. "And you didn't think you should include me in a decision like that?"

"Of course I did, but I knew you'd say no. And at that point, I knew I couldn't live with a no. I wanted a baby, and I was desperate and willing to do whatever it took to make that happen."

Even if what she'd done was wrong.

"My doctor told me I couldn't have any more eggs harvested for at least a year. Maybe not ever because I'd had a bad reaction to the fertility drugs." A reaction that'd almost killed her. "I figured one fertilized embryo was a long shot, but it was the only shot I had. So I hired a surrogate, Cissy Blanco, to carry Emily for me."

Reed cursed, groaned again. He opened his mouth, closed it and with his back against the wall, sank down onto the floor.

"I didn't tell you, because I knew how you felt about becoming a father," Addison added.

"You knew it, and yet you went through with this." His voice was raw and clipped, each one of his words punching into her like fists.

"I never expected you to be a father to the baby," she went on.

"But I fathered her!" he practically shouted. It was so loud that it startled Emily, and she started to whimper.

Addison pulled the baby closer to her and rocked her, hoping it would help, but it was possible that Emily was picking up on the tension in the room. There was certainly plenty enough of it to pick up on.

The door flew open again, and just like that, Reed was back in lawman mode. He pulled his gun and got to his feet. But it was just the nurse again. This time there was plenty of concern in her eyes.

"Is everything okay?" she asked. "I heard someone shouting."

"Everything's fine," Addison lied.

A burst of air left Reed's mouth. A laugh, but definitely not from humor. "My ex-wife and I were just having a little talk," he grumbled.

The nurse gave Addison a long look, no doubt silently asking if it was okay for her to leave, and Addison finally nodded. There was no need for an audience for the argument that Reed and she were about to continue having.

Once the nurse had left, Reed walked closer, staring down at Emily. Every muscle in his body was tight, the pulse in his throat throbbing.

"Are you going to ask if she's really yours?" Addison tossed out there.

The staring went on for several more long moments. "No."

Maybe he could see the resemblance. Emily had his

dark brown hair, and even though Emily's eyes were closed now, they were the same shade of deep blue as Reed's. There were times, like now, when Emily had that same intensity in her expression as Reed.

"I went to the storage facility with the nurse to pick up our embryo, and I was with the surrogate when it was implanted. If I'd thought I could harvest more eggs," Addison continued, "I wouldn't have used our embryo."

She would have used donor sperm with newly harvested eggs so that Reed wouldn't have been included in this process. Of course, her intentions meant nothing to him now. He'd just learned he was something he'd never truly wanted to be.

A father.

Nothing she could say to him would soothe that. Still, she tried.

"I didn't intend to tell you," she went on. "I knew all along this was my baby, not yours. I don't expect or want anything from you."

That sent a flash of anger through his eyes, but that anger faded when he looked at Emily. He reached down, brushed his finger over Emily's cheek and turned away. "She looks like my mother."

Addison wasn't sure if that was good or bad. Reed hadn't talked much about his folks, and she'd never met them. However, from what Addison had gathered, Reed had been physically abused by his alcoholic father and left alone after cancer finished off his mother. He would have ended up in foster care if it hadn't been for Roy McKinnon. Roy had taken him in when Reed was fourteen and raised him as his own, but by then the damage had been done, and Reed had wanted nothing to do with parenthood.

Damage that Addison had always thought she could undo and convince him that he would indeed make a wonderful father.

She'd failed big-time.

"Go ahead," Addison insisted. "Yell at me. Tell me how wrong I was to do this to you."

She braced herself for him to carry through on her offer, and maybe he strongly considered doing just that, but he glanced down at his badge. The thing that'd always anchored him.

"You hired a surrogate," Reed said. The emotion was still in his voice, but at least he wasn't yelling. "From this Dearborn Agency. I don't remember them coming up in the baby farm investigations, but it's possible they did."

That sent another chill through her even though it was something Addison had to consider. Those kidnappers had come after her for a reason, and the reason might have something to do with Dearborn or even the surrogate herself.

"I need to contact Cissy Blanco, the surrogate," Addison said. "To see if she knows anything about this."

"I'll contact her." Reed didn't leave any room for argument, either. He was taking charge of getting to the bottom of this. "Is it possible the surrogate developed a strong attachment to the baby and she didn't want to give Emily up?"

Addison was about to jump to say no, but then she remembered something. "I don't think she developed an attachment, but about midway through the pregnancy, something about Cissy changed. She was moody. Maybe even scared."

"Scared? About what?"

"There was a question about some mix-up with embryos, and the doctor at Dearborn gave Cissy an amnio test to make sure the baby she was carrying was ours. It was. But I think having the test was the start of her being upset."

"The start? There was more?" Reed snapped.

Addison nodded. "She'd mentioned being worried about her sister, who was also a surrogate at Dearborn, but when I brought it up again at our next visit, Cissy said everything was okay, that I should forget she even said anything about it. I blew it off, thinking she was just going through pregnancy hormones."

But Addison couldn't be sure of that now.

"Maybe not all of Dearborn's surrogates were legal," Reed said. "Maybe some of them were involved with the baby farms."

That put Addison's heart in her throat. Was that true? If so, it would perhaps explain why the attack had happened.

"We should do a DNA swab on Emily just in case the question of her paternity comes up," Reed suggested.

It wasn't even something she wanted to consider, and Addison had been there with Cissy for the in vitro procedure. She was positive Emily was Reed's and her baby. Still, Reed was right. They needed to have proof in case there were arrests made at Dearborn.

"When's the last time you had contact with Cissy?" he asked.

"Not since Emily was born seven weeks ago. I was in the delivery room with her, and a few hours afterward I went in to thank her again, but Cissy was already gone. She checked herself out of the hospital."

That got Reed's attention. "And you didn't think anything was wrong with that?"

Sadly, Addison had to shake her head again. "I wasn't thinking of anything but the baby. I sent the last of Cissy's payments to Dearborn and figured that was the end of it."

Of course, Addison hadn't even attempted to get in touch with the woman. In a way, she'd wanted to put the whole surrogacy behind her and get on with her new life. That could have turned out to be a mistake.

"What do I do now?" she asked, kissing Emily's forehead.

That got his muscles working hard again. "The baby and you will need protective custody until I can find out why those men came after you, and..." But his explanation ground to a halt. "I need a minute," he said, and reached for the door.

Addison figured it'd take a lot more than a minute for Reed to come to terms with what he'd just learned. Heck, maybe a lifetime wouldn't be enough. However, he hadn't even made it out of the room before his phone rang.

He glanced down at the screen, and when he pulled back his shoulders, Addison got up so she could see what'd caused that reaction.

Unknown caller.

"It could be just a telemarketer or wrong number," Reed reminded her.

Maybe, but after the hellish morning they'd had, Addison doubted it. Reed hit the answer button and put the call on speaker.

"Don't bother to trace this, cowboy," the caller said. "I'm using a burner cell." It wasn't a normal voice but had been disguised with a scrambler.

One of the kidnappers, no doubt.

"You need to tell your ex that this isn't over," the caller continued.

"Who are you and what do you want?" Reed demanded.

"Addison knows what we want. The names of everyone she told."

"Told what?" Addison said, rushing closer to get to the phone.

"*You know.* If you want to see what'll happen to you, then look at the surprise we left for you at your house."

"What surprise?" Reed and she asked together.

"You'll see," the voice taunted. "You're a dead woman, Addison, and this time that cowboy won't be able to save you."

Chapter Five

There was so much going on in Reed's head that he thought he might explode. How the devil had things gotten this crazy in such a short time?

He was a father.

Him!

Reed bit back another groan and tried to force himself to think. Not about Emily. Or Addison. Hard not to think about them, though, when the two were right in front of him, seated at his desk at the sheriff's office. Every time he looked at the baby's face, he was reminded that Addison had gone behind his back and done the very thing he hadn't wanted her to do. Still, his ex's betrayal had to go on the back burner for now.

Because of the threat.

"You're a dead woman, Addison, and this time that cowboy won't be able to save you."

That in itself was bad enough, but there was the kidnapper's other comment about the surprise at Addison's house. Or rather what was left of her place. According to Colt, who was on the scene, the place had indeed been burned to the ground.

"I can't get a good look at the rubble yet," Colt said from the other end of the line. "The fire department's still hosing it down."

Both Colt and Reed cursed. For a good reason. The water was necessary to make sure the fire didn't spread, but it would also likely destroy any evidence. Of course, there might not be any evidence to find.

The *surprise* could just be an empty threat. A ploy to put the fear of God into Addison. If so, it was working.

"Anything?" Addison asked the moment Reed ended the call with Colt. As she had been doing once they arrived at the sheriff's office, she was nibbling on her bottom lip. Clearly panicked by all this.

Not Emily, though.

Now that she'd finished her bottle, the baby was sleeping in Addison's arms. Even though Reed had said he wouldn't focus on the little girl now, it was hard to ignore the tiny bundle that was causing such an avalanche of emotions inside him.

She was his daughter.

They'd done the DNA test, just in case her paternity came up, but Reed was certain what the test results would be.

"Nothing yet," Reed answered. "But if there's anything to find in the house, Colt will find it."

He hoped. They had enough unanswered questions without adding this so-called threat to the list.

Cooper and the other deputy, Pete Nichols, were on their phones trying to track down that black SUV so Reed figured he'd better push aside the emotional avalanche and get to work on other things.

Like finding a safe place for Addison and Emily.

He seriously doubted she wanted to spend the rest of the day at the sheriff's office. Or with him for that matter. But Reed couldn't let her out of his sight until he knew both Emily and she would be safe.

"Why is this happening?" Addison asked on a rise of breath.

That was one of the big questions on Reed's mind, too. So he sank down in the chair across from her to see if they could come up with something, anything that would help him catch the people responsible for this.

Of course, first he had to figure out what *this* was.

"I don't believe the kidnappers actually wanted the baby," Reed said, testing a theory that he'd been tossing around in his head with all the other jumbled thoughts. Maybe if he talked it out with her, it'd make more sense. "I believe they only took her to get you to cooperate with them. Think about it. They handed her to me, but they were going to take you."

Addison's eyes widened. "You're right. It's me they're after."

The kidnappers probably hadn't wanted to have to take care of a newborn. That's why they'd intended to make such a fast trade of Addison for the baby. Now that their plan had failed, they probably wouldn't hesitate to use the baby to get Addison again.

But Reed didn't intend to let them do that.

"Cooper ran a check on the baby farm investigation, and the Dearborn Agency didn't come up," Reed continued. "But there were some surrogates in the baby farms that have been found and interviewed. Ones who'd been hired by less than sterling prospective parents. In some cases the surrogates had been kidnapped, or at least pretended to be kidnapped, and the babies held for ransom from the couples who'd hired them."

"You honestly think some of the surrogates were in on a scheme like that?" Addison asked.

"Possibly. Did Cissy try to get any extra money from you?"

Addison quickly shook her head. "No." Then she paused. "But she knew I'd used most of my savings to pay for the surrogacy. And I didn't inherit my aunt's house until the week after Emily was born."

That was right. Reed remembered it'd been held up in probate court for nearly a year because Addison's aunt hadn't left a will. Addison had eventually been given the house after it was determined that she was her aunt's only legitimate heir, but neither anyone at Dearborn nor Cissy would have known for certain Addison was getting the place.

"Besides, if milking more money from me was the motive, then why wait seven weeks after the probate court's ruling?" Addison asked. "Why not just kidnap Emily then and demand a ransom?"

Those were the reasons Reed had dismissed that particular part of the theory, too. But it brought him back to the surrogate angle itself.

"Even though Dearborn didn't come up in the investigation, they could have been involved with the baby farms. They'd probably do anything to make sure the surrogate doesn't say a word to you about the baby farm operation."

Addison gave a quick nod. "We have to find out who owns the Dearborn Agency."

"I'm working on that," Cooper said, sliding his hand over the phone receiver. "So far, it's like digging through a very big haystack."

Oh, man. That wasn't good at all. People with nothing to hide generally put their names on businesses they owned.

Cooper opened his mouth to add something to that, but he stopped, his gaze going to the glass door. Reed whirled in that direction to see what'd gotten the sheriff's attention, and he immediately spotted the two men making their way from the parking lot.

Not the kidnappers, but Reed didn't recognize them, so he slid his hand over his gun.

The man in the lead was tall and thin with dark hair. He was wearing a bright blue suit that was fitted close enough to his body that Reed didn't think he was carrying concealed. However, he could have a weapon in the briefcase gripped in his hand.

The other man was a different story. Early forties. Bulky around the middle, and he was wearing a coat over his suit jacket. Plenty of places for him to hide a weapon.

"It's Rooney, the P.I., and my attorney, Dominic Harrelson," Addison said, getting to her feet.

She clutched Emily even tighter to her. That body language didn't cause Reed to relax any, and he kept his hand on his gun.

"Good." Cooper stood, too. "I called them both and told them to get in here."

Reed stepped in front of the baby and Addison when the pair stepped into the building. Cooper and Pete moved next to him, all three protecting Addison just in case one or both of their visitors turned out to be a threat.

"Addison," Dominic said, his attention going straight to her. He would have walked to Addison if Reed hadn't blocked his path. "Are you all right? It's all over the news about the kidnapping attempt."

"We're okay," Addison answered.

Dominic flinched, maybe surprised Addison hadn't given him a warmer greeting. Or maybe because Addison had stayed behind Reed. Of course, that nasty bruise on Addison's forehead might have something to do with Dominic's response, too, because along with the kidnapping attempt, it was obvious that Addison wasn't anywhere close to being *okay*.

"You wanted to see me," Rooney said, extending his hand first to Reed, then to Cooper. Reed kept his grip on his gun, but Cooper shook hands with the P.I.

"Did you two come together?" Reed asked, just so he'd know if these two were chummy or not. He definitely wasn't picking up on any friendly vibes, but he wanted to know the dynamics here before they got started with the questions about the investigation.

"No," Rooney assured him. "I've taken a hotel room here in town, and we just happened to drive up at the same time."

Reed hoped that was a coincidence, and one wasn't following the other. Of course, at this point, he suspected nearly everybody of doing something wrong. Hard to rid his mind of that possibility after what'd happened.

"I understand Addison hired you to do some background checks," Reed said to the P.I.

Judging from the surprise in his eyes, Dominic didn't know about that, and judging from Rooney's scowl, this wasn't something he wanted to discuss with Reed or Dominic.

Tough.

Rooney was discussing it.

"It's okay," Addison assured the P.I. "I've told Reed and Sheriff McKinnon everything."

Everything, including the fact that Reed was a father. But again, he shoved that thought aside.

"Background checks?" Dominic questioned. "On who?"

"You, for one," Rooney readily admitted. He shucked

off his overcoat, then his jacket, but the P.I.'s shirt was still bulky enough to have hidden a gun. Which he probably had. After all, Rooney had a license to carry a concealed weapon.

"A background check on me?" Dominic snapped.

Addison nodded. "The Dearborn Agency, too. After all the news about the baby farms, I thought I should just make sure everything was aboveboard," she added, though Dominic's mouth had dropped open.

"You thought I had something to do with all that baby farm mess?" Dominic continued, and after glaring at Addison and Rooney, he turned to Cooper. "I didn't. I was Addison's attorney for the surrogacy agreement, that's all."

"I'd like to see the agreement," Reed said quickly.

There'd been a lot of color in Dominic's cheeks, but some of that color faded after Reed's demand.

"The agreement was stolen, right?" Rooney asked.

Dominic nodded. "I'm not sure when it happened. I looked for it after the sheriff called, but it wasn't there."

Not that Reed needed proof this was a bad situation, but if he did, that was it. Reed turned to the P.I. "How'd you know it'd been stolen?"

"I guessed, that's how. Someone stole all the surrogate files from Dearborn, too. They also ransacked Addison's apartment. I found that out on the drive over." Rooney shifted his attention to her. "The San Antonio cops will be calling you soon about it."

"Sweet heaven," Addison mumbled. "The kidnappers likely took the copy from my aunt's house, too."

Yeah, and even by some miracle they'd missed it, the fire would have destroyed it. Someone wanted to be thorough about this, which made Reed wonder what exactly was in that surrogacy agreement.

Someone obviously had something to hide.

But what, exactly?

"What about the surrogate Addison hired? Any chance she could be involved in this?" Cooper asked.

"No," Dominic said as Rooney answered, "Possibly."

Reed gave each of them an *explain that* look.

It was Dominic who continued first. "I read a report on Cissy and several of the other surrogate possibilities from Dearborn. There was nothing in any of their reports to indicate criminal activity on her part." Then he shook his head and lifted his shoulder. "Of course, someone could have falsified the reports I read."

The lawyer was right. And heck, maybe it wasn't just the report that was fake. It was possible that Cissy Blanco wasn't even the surrogate's real name.

"I'm on it," Cooper volunteered, and he headed back to his desk, no doubt to make calls about the surrogate.

"You think Cissy was *possibly* involved in this," Reed said to Rooney.

Even though the room wasn't that warm, there were beads of sweat on his face, and Rooney wiped them away with the back of his hand. "I don't have anything specific, but something's not right with the Dearborn Agency itself."

It meshed with what Cooper had said, too. "What have you found?" Reed pressed.

"That's just it. I haven't found much of anything. It's a corporation, but it's buried under layers of paperwork, and I can't find out who actually owns it. When I asked the office manager about the owner and the board of directors, all I got was the runaround."

That brought Addison out from behind him, but she turned toward Dominic, not Rooney. "And you didn't know any of this?"

Dominic threw up his hands. "Why would I? You contacted Dearborn before you ever asked me to do the surrogacy agreement. I just assumed you had vetted them and trusted them."

Reed looked at Addison to see if that was true. Apparently, it was. "A woman at the fertility clinic I used recommended Dearborn. So did my fertility specialist. I hired Dominic to make sure there were no holes or discrepancies in the contract I had to sign with them."

It was a smart move on Addison's part so she could ensure that she actually got the baby if the surrogate managed to become pregnant. However, the discrepancies might not be with the contract but with the agency itself.

Or with the lawyer who'd blessed the agreement.

"Who do you think tried to kidnap Addison?" Reed asked.

However, before their visitors could answer, a sound distracted Reed. Emily's soft whimper. When he looked back at the baby, he realized she was staring at him. Studying him as he'd done to her earlier. Reed didn't want to feel anything, not right now anyway, when he had so many questions to ask their visitors.

But he did.

He felt as if someone had knocked the breath right out of him. And maybe someone had. *Emily.* That tiny baby bundled in Addison's arms had nearly brought him to his knees.

"Are you all right?" Addison whispered.

No, he wasn't, far from it, but he needed to finish these interviews so he could sit down and try to process everything that'd happened.

Reed must have looked sick to his stomach, because Rooney took out a foil roll of antacids from his pocket and offered him one. When Reed shook his head, declining, Rooney popped two of them into his own mouth.

"I'm not sure exactly what's going on here," Rooney concluded, "but I don't want to be caught up in the blame game. For the record, I only did the job that Addison hired me to do, and I'll continue doing it unless she tells me to stop."

"You might want to rethink that. All of this could be dangerous," Addison said. Not exactly firing the man, but the warning was definitely warranted.

"Yeah, I'm gettin' that. Kidnapping attempts, your place burned down and it all seems to lead back to either you..." He motioned toward Dominic before putting his thumb against his own chest. "Me. Or Dearborn. My money's on the agency."

Addison shook her head. "But who in the agency? The only person I dealt with there was the office manager, Donna Cannon."

"She's gone," Rooney explained. "She quit about a month ago, and they've been using a temp ever since."

Well, that explained why Cooper wasn't getting a lot of answers. "Who do you think is behind Dearborn?" Reed asked.

"Gunther Quarles," Rooney said without hesitation.

Dominic looked at the P.I. as if he'd gone mad. "Quarles is a judge."

Reed knew the name. Not just a judge but a rich, respected one. In addition to his being a judge, Quarles's family had a charity foundation for underprivileged kids.

"I know exactly what he is," Rooney said. "But I don't like the way his name keeps popping up in my investigation. He signed at least five of the recent adoption decrees from Dearborn."

Now it was Reed's turn to shrug. "I'd imagine he's signed dozens of decrees like that. It's his job."

"I thought that at first, too, but if you dig a little deeper, you'll find at least three of the birth mothers were teenagers and had spent some time in facilities run by Quarles's foundation."

"That doesn't mean anything, either," Dominic insisted. The attorney had never looked comfortable with this interview, but his discomfort went up a significant notch. He fingered his collar and then moved those fidgety fingers to the back of his neck. "It's not a good idea to antagonize a man like Quarles."

The lawyer checked the time on his phone. "I have another appointment." Dominic spared Addison a glance. "I'll be in touch."

Reed moved in front of Dominic when he reached for the door. "Sorry, but I'll need both you and Rooney to stay and give statements. We need to find out everything you know about this investigation."

Dominic huffed. "But I've already told you everything."

"Then you won't mind writing it down." Reed didn't give either of them a chance to refuse, either. He pointed toward the two interview rooms just up the hall. "Rooney on the right. Dominic, you can take the left one."

Rooney headed in the direction he'd been instructed, clearly cooperating. About this anyway. But Reed had been a deputy long enough to know that sometimes the most cooperative suspects were the guiltiest. Rooney could be here to manipulate the investigation or at least try to figure out what Reed knew.

Which wasn't much.

Reed would have to do something fast about his lack

of information, but first on his agenda was finding that safe house for Addison and the baby.

Pete and Cooper followed the P.I. and the lawyer into the rooms. Maybe they'd be able to get more out of them while they wrote up their statements.

"I'm really sorry about this," Addison whispered the moment that Dominic and Rooney were out of earshot.

He was still riled about her going through with the surrogacy without telling him, but Reed figured Addison had more than enough to deal with right now. He managed a nod, brushed his hand on her arm and reached for his phone so he could start making those safe-house arrangements.

However, the phone rang, and when Reed saw Colt's name on the screen, he answered right away and put the call on speaker so Addison could hear.

"The firemen finally put out the fire," Colt said immediately. But his hesitation after that had Reed groaning.

"What's wrong now?" Addison asked.

"The kidnappers weren't lying. They left something in the house." Again, Colt hesitated. "It's a body."

Chapter Six

A body.

Because her legs felt as if they were about to give way, Addison sank back down into the chair. It was a good thing she was holding Emily, because her baby was the only reason she didn't lose it then and there.

Reed took the call off speaker, probably because he could see how upset she was, and he continued the conversation with Colt. Addison figured with the way things had been going, it was too much to ask that this was some kind of accidental death.

No.

Those kidnappers had almost certainly killed someone and put the body in her house. Some kind of sick warning to go along with that equally sick threat.

"You're a dead woman, Addison, and this time that cowboy won't be able to save you."

No, but Reed would try to do just that—save her. She wanted to find someone else to do it. Anyone else. But the truth was that Reed was her best shot right now when it came to keeping Emily safe. Even though he was still plenty uncertain about fatherhood, he would do whatever it took to keep the baby out of harm's way.

Maybe it would be enough.

Reed finished his call with Colt, and he went to the

interview room that held Cooper and Pete. Both the sheriff and the other deputy stepped out in the hall, and Reed had a whispered conversation with them. She couldn't hear what was being said, but whatever it was prompted Pete and Cooper to make phone calls. Reed, too.

When Reed came back into the squad room, he took hold of her arm and helped her stand.

"Whose body is it?" Addison asked, though she wasn't sure she could even handle the answer right now.

He shook his head. "It might take a while to determine that. Come on, I'm getting you out of here."

Addison pulled back her shoulder. "Is it safe to do that?"

"I'll make it safe," Reed assured her.

He picked up the diaper bag that she'd gotten from the hospital. All of Emily's things had been destroyed in the fire, but the nurses had managed to get some diapers, wipes, baby gowns and formula for her.

With the bag hooked over his shoulder, Reed led her toward the back exit. Not alone, either. Pete stepped out from the room with Dominic to follow them.

"I called in the other deputies and alerted the ranch hands," Pete told Reed. The deputy kept his voice practically at a whisper. "Jasper's heading over there now to make sure everything's okay. If there's a problem, he'll call you. Shawna's coming in to help Cooper with the statements."

Jasper Willett and Shawna Davidson. Addison knew both of them well. Normally, they were the night deputies, but it was obvious this wasn't a normal situation. She welcomed any and all help.

"Where are we going?" she asked Reed.

"Sweetwater Ranch." A muscle flickered in his jaw.

Probably because he knew she wouldn't be comfortable going to Roy McKinnon's home.

And she wasn't. "Roy—"

"He's okay with it."

Maybe. But that was only the tip of the iceberg. "What about the others? Cooper has a toddler, and his wife's pregnant. His sister Rayanne is, too. And his other sister, Rosalie, has a baby. They all live on the ranch grounds and can't possibly want me bringing danger right to their doorstep."

"It's all being taken care of," Reed insisted, which could have meant anything. "Move fast when we're in the parking lot."

Despite her reservations about this plan, she did just that. Addison didn't want to be outside in the open any longer than Reed obviously did. He got them in his truck, and she strapped Emily into the car seat the nurses had also given her. The second she finished doing that, Reed got them out of there. Pete was right behind them in a police car.

"We're going to the guesthouse on the McKinnons' ranch," Reed told her while he checked all around them. No doubt to make sure they weren't being followed. Addison did some checking of her own, and she kept her arm over Emily's car seat in case she had to react fast.

"The guesthouse? But isn't the ranch where Jewell's stepson is staying?" That was what Addison had heard anyway. That Jewell's stepson, Seth, was staying in Sweetwater Springs to be closer to Jewell, the woman who'd raised him, and Jewell had insisted he stay in the guesthouse.

Reed nodded. "He'll be there until Jewell's trial, but he's away on an investigation right now. Roy agreed that it's okay if we use the place."

Good. That was better than the main house where Roy would be. Of course, she doubted she'd be able to avoid all the male McKinnons, but maybe she wouldn't have to be there that long.

"What about the plans for a safe house?" she asked.

"Still working on that." Reed didn't get a chance to add more, because his phone buzzed. Emily was between them, but Addison still caught a glimpse of the screen.

Gunther Quarles, the judge.

Addison doubted this call was a coincidence. "Put it on speaker," she insisted. "I want to hear what he has to say."

Guessing from the look Reed gave her, he debated that a couple of seconds, but then he did as she asked.

"This is Deputy Caldwell," Reed answered. He put the phone on his lap, no doubt so he could keep his hands free in case he had to reach for his gun. After all, this call could be some kind of ploy to distract them. "How can I help you, Judge Quarles?"

"You can tell me what's going on. I understand my name came up in conversation today at the Sweetwater Springs Sheriff's Office."

Reed huffed, clearly not happy that Quarles had already learned that. "It did. But how did you know about it?"

"Someone gave me a heads-up. I'd rather not say who exactly."

She seriously doubted Cooper would have phoned the judge yet, so the heads-up had likely come from either Rooney or Dominic. Dominic had been the one to defend Quarles, so Addison was betting he had done it.

But why had her lawyer called the judge anyway?

Were they friends? Or did Dominic feel as if he owed Quarles in some way?

"I just wanted you to know I'm sorry about the attack on your ex-wife," Quarles went on. "That was horrible, just horrible. I had nothing to do with it, of course, and I really don't want my name tossed around with accusations of wrongdoing."

"And who is it that accused you of wrongdoing?" Reed asked, probably to see just how much Quarles had been told.

Quarles's huff was plenty loud enough for her to hear it. "I don't want to play games with you, Deputy. You know what was said about me and who said it. Now it'll stop. I'm calling Sheriff McKinnon next to make sure no other accusations come my way."

"Did you have anything to do with the attack or the baby farms?" Reed pressed.

Quarles didn't jump to deny it, but Addison could almost feel the anger seeping from the other end of the line. "You have no idea who you're dealing with," the judge finally said.

"I'm dealing with a judge whose name came up in conversation in regards to the baby farms and the attack on my ex-wife and a baby," Reed fired back. "I'm a little testy right now after being shot at and all, but I intend to find out the truth about what happened today."

"Good luck with that," Quarles snapped, and he hung up.

Addison figured she should be troubled that they'd just upset a powerful judge with a surly attitude, but she was more concerned that Quarles could possibly be a part of this. Until she knew who was responsible for the danger, and why, Emily would never be safe.

"I'll do some checking on Quarles," Reed said as he put his phone away. "Maybe something will turn up."

It was a generous offer, considering that Quarles could try to hurt Reed's career, but she figured if the judge was involved in the baby farms or the attack today, then he would have hidden that connection so well that it'd be nearly impossible to find. Still, Quarles appeared to have a short fuse, so maybe he would trip up and reveal something incriminating.

Sooner or later, something had to go in their favor.

She hoped.

"What happens if we don't find out who's behind this?" Addison hated to ask, but she needed to know.

Reed made a face as if insulted by that, and he tapped his badge. "Believe me, I'll find out."

Coming from any other man, that would have sounded cocky, but Reed was a good lawman. Addison prayed that *good* would be good enough.

His gaze drifted to Emily, staying on her for just a few seconds before he went back to looking around. "She sleeps a lot."

"Only during the day." Addison was only partly joking about that. "If you hope to get any sleep tonight, you'll need to put some distance between you and us."

"No distance," he answered quickly. "We'll all be in the same bedroom."

Of course they would be. She should have already realized that Reed wouldn't risk letting her out of his sight. The baby would be there with them so it wasn't as if Reed and she would actually be alone. In a bedroom. Still, her body seemed to think they would be, and the memories came flooding back.

Memories of so many other times when Reed and she had been alone and in bed.

Despite the hellish ordeal they'd just been through, Addison felt that familiar trickle of heat seep through her. The kind of heat only Reed could generate inside her. Yes, their marriage had failed big-time, but no matter what she did to try to cool it down, the attraction was still there. Probably always would be.

Something that didn't exactly please her.

Reed took the turn toward the Sweetwater Ranch, and she saw the sprawling pastures, houses and outbuildings. More memories came.

Some good, some bad.

Addison had lived in Sweetwater Springs most of her life, first with her parents in a house not too far from here. Then, when her folks had been killed in a car accident when she was sixteen, she moved in to her aunt's place only about ten miles away. By then, Reed had been living with the McKinnons, so Addison had seen him often enough. They hadn't dated because of the four-year age difference, though, until she'd come back after college.

And then they'd gotten married in the McKinnon house.

Addison got another dose of those memories when they drove past it.

"This is the safest place I could think of," Reed reminded her, probably sensing that she wasn't at all comfortable with this arrangement. After all, they were returning to the scene of the start of their failed marriage.

He stopped his truck in front of the small guest cottage just across the yard from the main house. There were ranch hands milling around. All armed. No doubt there to protect Emily and her. Too bad they might be needed, especially since she had no idea if a ranch this large could even be secured.

She adjusted the blanket around Emily, and they got out, hurrying into the cottage. The place was small, just as she remembered. A living-kitchen combo area, two bedrooms and a shared bath between them. There was also an infant basket on the coffee table, more diapers and some baby clothes.

"Rosalie brought the stuff over," Reed explained.

Good. Addison made a mental note to thank her later. Along with Jewell, Addison had kept in touch with Jewell's twin daughters over the years, and both women were grateful that Addison was willing to help their mother by being a character witness at Jewell's trail.

There'd be no such gratitude from Jewell's sons, however.

Colt, Tucker and Cooper didn't want Addison or anyone else to say anything at their mother's murder trial that would implicate their father. Addison had no intention of doing that, mainly because she knew nothing that would implicate Roy. Still, there had been a line drawn in the proverbial sand here, and Addison was on the wrong side of that line when it came to the McKinnon males.

And Reed.

Of course, Reed and she were on opposite sides now for a different reason. Their failed marriage. And now the baby.

"Are we going to talk about Emily?" she asked, easing the baby into the basket.

"No." As if angry with it, Reed twisted the locks on the door and punched in the numbers to set the security system. Then he huffed. "There's nothing to talk about, really."

She hadn't meant to make a loud sound of surprise.

"Really?" Addison said. "I know you're upset."

"That doesn't mean we have to talk about it." Reed turned toward the kitchen but then just as quickly whirled back around to face her. "All right, let's talk," he snapped.

Even though Addison had wanted to go ahead and get this out in the open, Reed's suddenly intense expression had her wanting to take a step back. She didn't. Addison figured she deserved it if he lashed out at her.

But he didn't lash out.

A weary sigh left his mouth, and much to her further surprise, Reed reached out and pulled her into his arms. "I just need time to work out all this in my head."

Addison wasn't sure what exactly he needed to work out, but it set off another alarm inside her. One not just associated with the reminder of being in his arms. She eased back so she could look him in the eye.

Not exactly a good decision on her part.

For a moment she got lost in those eyes. His mouth. And she couldn't let it happen. Reed and she had too many things to settle without adding *that* to the mix. And that was why Addison stepped away from him.

"I made the decision to have Emily," she said. "That doesn't mean I expect you to be her father. In fact, I'd rather you not be."

Okay, that didn't come out right, and it created a whole new fire in Reed's eyes. This time, she didn't think the physical attraction between them had anything to do with it.

No, she'd riled him to the core.

"When you filed for the divorce," she tried again, "I knew I had to forget about you. I made plans for a life without you. A life as a single parent."

They hadn't been easy plans, but she'd made them all right. Addison didn't want to open up herself to that again. She'd barely survived the breakup with Reed the last time, and she wasn't sure she could survive another heart stomping. Even if that stomping had been justified.

"So you're saying, you'll cut me out of Emily's life?" Reed tossed out there.

"You're saying you want to be part of her life?" But Addison waved him off before he could answer. His answer might not be something she could take right now. Not with her already frazzled nerves. "I don't expect you to understand."

"Then go ahead, spell it out for me," he insisted.

This was ancient history. With some god-awful painful parts. "You know I've always wanted a child. A family," she corrected. "A shrink would probably say it's because of the guilt that I feel over losing my baby sister when I was ten years old."

It was, in part. She didn't need a shrink to confirm it, either.

Addison was supposed to have been watching her six-year-old sister, Hannah. Something that she'd griped about doing because she had wanted to watch a show on TV. Addison hadn't been paying close enough attention when the little girl had ridden her bike out onto the road and was hit by a car.

You couldn't make up for that kind of loss, Addison had soon learned. Her parents had never forgiven her.

Well, they had with words.

But she'd always seen the grief and lack of forgiveness in their eyes, and they'd been killed six years later when their truck skidded off an icy bridge. Because of their deaths, there'd be no chance of redemption for her.

No family.

The loss had been bone-deep and had stayed with her all these years later. It would for the rest of her life.

"I always wanted to have a family," she reminded him, "to make up for the one I lost, and you don't want a family you never had."

"I had a family," he corrected, his voice edged with anger. "Not a good one, but Roy was more than enough of a father to me to make up for that."

Oh, so they were back to that. "And now you think I'm hurting Roy by testifying for Jewell?"

"Aren't you?"

Yes, they were definitely back to that. "I'm only telling the truth. I don't think Jewell's capable of murder. Over the past ten years or so, Jewell and I have had plenty of conversations and visits. She's told me very personal things about her life, and not once has she ever mentioned killing a man. However, what she also hasn't done is rule out Roy as Whitt Braddock's killer. Roy had just as much motive as Jewell did to want Whitt dead."

That got Reed's jaw muscles working against each other.

"Then we'll agree to disagree." Reed's attention landed on Emily again. "But that doesn't apply to her. She's my daughter, and I *will* be in her life."

Addison flinched. That sounded like a threat. However, before she could ask Reed exactly what he meant by that, his phone buzzed. Even though it wasn't loud, it was enough to wake up Emily, and the baby immediately started to fuss. Addison went to her while Reed took out his phone.

"It's Colt," he let her know.

Reed didn't put the call on speaker, so Addison could only wait and watch to see what was going on. Judging from the way his forehead bunched up, this was yet another dose of bad news. Unfortunately, she couldn't tell what kind of bad news. Reed was only listening and not asking any questions.

"What's wrong?" she asked the moment he finished the call.

"Colt's still out at your aunt's place." He pulled in a long breath. "They got an I.D. on the body."

Chapter Seven

Cissy Blanco.

Reed sat at the small kitchen table of the guest cottage and studied the surrogate's file that Cooper had emailed him earlier. Cissy was young, barely twenty-two. Blond hair, brown eyes. She'd had a run-in with the law when she was a juvenile but nothing since.

And now she was dead.

Her body partially burned in the fire that'd destroyed Addison's house.

However, the fire hadn't been the cause of Cissy's death. A bullet to the head had seen to that, and then her body had apparently been dumped in the house. Along with her I.D. in her pocket. There was only one reason Reed could think of for her killer to do that

Because the killer wanted the law, and Addison, to know the dead woman's identity.

This had been a sick warning directed at Addison that she could be next if she didn't cooperate with Cissy's killers.

"Addison knows what we want. The names of everyone she told," the kidnapper had said when he called using that fake voice.

The kidnapper/killer probably thought Addison had included Cissy in that list of names. But told the surrogate what exactly? According to Addison, there was nothing to tell.

The killer clearly thought otherwise.

Addison had thought so, too. Well, she'd mentioned it in between her sobs about Cissy. Too bad she didn't know what bits of information she shouldn't have spilled. But even without knowing what if anything she'd said or done wrong, Addison blamed herself for Cissy's death. However, Reed put the blame right back on the killer.

Whoever that was.

This had to be linked to the surrogate herself and maybe even the Dearborn Agency. There was just one problem with that—neither Reed nor Colt had been able to find anything that would put a black mark on the agency. Yes, Cissy's surrogate file from Dearborn had been stolen or destroyed, but someone could have broken into Dearborn and taken it and any other files possibly connected to the baby farms. It didn't mean the agency itself was the culprit.

Reed read through the latest email that Cooper had sent him. Definitely not good info there, but what did it mean exactly?

And why the devil did Quarles's name keep coming up in this investigation?

Reed didn't have time to speculate about that any longer. He heard the sound in the bedroom, and he hurried there to make sure everything was okay. He'd left the door open. Left Addison and Emily sleeping, too. Since none of them had gotten much sleep during the night, he'd figured they would stay in bed until midmorning. But Emily was wide-awake, fussing, and Addison was fumbling to get out of bed.

"I'll get her bottle," she mumbled.

He knew for a fact Addison wasn't a morning person so Reed was a little surprised that she could move so fast. She picked up the basket with Emily still inside and made her way toward the kitchen. However, she did stumble, knocking her shoulder against the doorjamb.

For a sleep-starved, half-awake woman who'd been crying half the night, Addison still caught his attention in a bad way. Maybe it was the bulky T-shirt that managed to swallow her and hug her curves all at the same time. Or maybe it was the way her hair tumbled onto her shoulders. All mussed, as if she'd just had a long night of lovemaking instead of baby tending.

Of course, Addison always had a way of causing him to notice her, and he'd spent most of the night in the sleeping bag next to her trying not to notice that he was noticing.

That was just one of the reasons for his lack of sleep. The other had been the investigation weighing on his mind. Another had been the baby who was at the moment making him fully aware of her presence.

Emily's whimpers soon turned to a full-fledged cry when Addison set the basket on the table next to the laptop where Reed had been working.

"Need some help?" he asked Addison when she nearly dropped the bottle she'd picked up off the counter.

She shook her head, yawned and winced as if she had a headache. And maybe she did after the beating she'd taken the day before. "Don't worry. Emily will hush crying when she has her bottle."

No doubt, but in the meantime, she kept on crying. For something smaller than a sack of potatoes, Emily could sure make some noise.

"Sorry," Addison added. "I'm hurrying."

"No worries. The crying doesn't bother me."

Addison gave him another of those funny looks. She probably thought he was lying. But it honestly didn't bother him.

The sound of crying usually didn't.

Maybe because he'd heard his mother sob regularly and for long stints when he was kid. The cancer and the treatments had been pretty brutal, and there'd been a lot of tears.

Ironic, though, that he hadn't learned to hate the tears as much as he had the dangerous treatments she'd suffered to extend her life. Treatments that had ultimately failed, and her dying breath had been filled with yet more painful sobs.

Addison cursed when she spilled some of the formula she was pouring into the bottle. He considered offering to help her, but since he didn't have a clue about bottle making, Reed went to the basket instead. He was out of his element with the baby, too, but he jiggled the basket, hoping it would soothe her.

It didn't.

The kid likely had a good career ahead as a heavy metal singer judging from the way she was belting out those high notes.

Because the crying was obviously fraying Addison's nerves, Reed reached into the basket and picked up Emily. Of course, it wasn't the first time he'd held her. The kidnapper had handed off Emily to him when they were out on the road. But he'd thought he was holding Addison's adopted baby then.

Now he was holding his daughter.

The air and the room were suddenly so still that it felt as if everything had stopped and was waiting for his reaction. That didn't take long. Reed felt his heart thud against his chest. Felt the air race from his lungs.

Oh, man.

He'd expected a punch, but he hadn't expected *this*. The flood of emotions. That urgent need to protect this screaming little bundle.

"You don't have to do that," Addison said, suddenly sounding very wide-awake. She hurried to him and took Emily from his arms.

Emily chose that moment to stop crying, and the little girl volleyed looks at both of them, maybe trying to figure out why the tension in the room had just gone up a significant notch.

"Her bottle's ready," Addison added, almost like an apology. She sank down into one of the chairs and started feeding her. The baby was definitely hungry because the cries stopped, and she gobbled up the formula.

"Remember that conversation we had yesterday?" Reed asked Addison, but he didn't wait for her to remember something he was darn sure she hadn't forgotten. "I said I don't want you to try to shut her out of my life."

"I'm not trying to shut you out," Addison snapped. She huffed, shoved her hair away from her face. "Okay, maybe I am, but for the past year I've had to figure out how to get on without you. And I managed it. Now here we are again, together under the same roof and at each other's throats."

She probably hadn't meant that as some kind of sexual reference, but that was the direction Reed's mind went. It was yet another mental nudge he needed because the last place his mind should be going was *there*.

"Don't worry," he said to Addison. "I'll give you some time to get used to me being around again."

Heck, that sounded sexual, too, and Reed figured it

was a good time to just shut up and get back to work. It wasn't as if he didn't have plenty to do.

Huffing, Reed sat back down and started going through the emails that'd been coming in all night.

"Anything yet on Cissy's death?" Addison asked, drawing his attention back to her.

Not that his attention had strayed far.

When his mind wasn't on Addison and that blasted body-hugging T-shirt, it was on Emily. The baby girl looked so innocent and precious sucking her bottle, but she kept glancing at him from the corner of her eye. Maybe trying to figure out who he was exactly.

Heck, Reed was trying to figure that out, too.

Was he an idiot to think he should be in a little baby's life?

Nothing about him was father material, *nothing,* and he'd never felt the desire to pass on his less than stellar DNA to an innocent child. Still, there was this mountain-high pile of feelings he couldn't ignore. It didn't seem to matter that he didn't want to be a father.

The only thing that mattered now was that he was one.

"I'm going to suck at this," he said in a whisper.

Addison's gaze darted to his. "At finding Cissy's killer?"

He gave her a flat look, his own gaze going to Emily.

"Oh," Addison said, looking more uncomfortable about that than she would have had it been about the investigation.

That was something Addison and he would have to work on later. For now, Reed had to deal with the subject that might indeed bring Addison back to tears.

Cissy's murder.

"Cissy's sister, Mellie, reported her missing two days ago," Reed informed her. "Did you know?"

Addison shook her head, and yeah, the tears came again. While Emily's crying for a bottle hadn't bothered him too much, Addison's sure did.

"Cooper's heading out to talk to Mellie this morning, but he said that she's afraid. Rightfully so, after what happened to her sister."

He added some profanity when Addison's tears continued to fall, and Reed stood to get her a paper towel.

"Thanks," she said. "Did Mellie have any idea who murdered Cissy?"

"No." Reed sat down again so he could face Addison for the rest of this. "But Mellie was a surrogate, too, at Dearborn, and she said that she's pretty sure someone's been following her."

"Oh, God." The color drained from Addison's face. "You have to protect her—"

"We will. Cooper's sending someone from the San Antonio Police Department out to the address Dearborn had on file for her." He paused to give Addison a moment to gather her breath. Heck, he needed a moment to catch his, too. "Did anything go on at Dearborn that you haven't told me?"

"No." Another quick denial. "It wasn't like the baby farms. Cissy was a willing surrogate, and I paid her. She wasn't being held against her will. If she had been, she would have had plenty of chances to tell me."

That didn't mean Cissy hadn't kept secrets. Secrets that had in turn gotten her killed. After all, they didn't know the full extent of the baby farms and what had gone on at any of them. Dearborn itself could have been part of the operation.

"You said there was only one of our embryos left,"

Reed started. "I remember the doctors trying to implant two or more when you had in vitro done. Only one wouldn't have a high chance of success."

"No," she agreed, studying him. "What are you asking?"

He was about to ask a question that was going to bring up a lot of bad blood between them. "Did you have any experimental treatments done to help you produce more eggs you didn't tell me about?"

"You mean treatments like the one that nearly killed me? No," she grumbled, not waiting for him to answer. "I didn't."

Yeah, definitely bad blood. Enough that it had caused their separation. After Addison had healed, that is. The experimental treatments had jacked up her blood pressure to the point she'd nearly had a stroke.

She'd nearly killed herself.

Just as his mother had, going from one treatment to another. Reed had long made peace with his mother's choice because she was dying anyway. But Addison, well, there'd been no peace with that yet. She'd been a reasonably healthy woman who had chosen to do some very unhealthy things to her body to up her chances of getting pregnant. Chances that her own doctors had told her weren't likely to work anyway.

"I got lucky with just the one embryo," Addison added a moment later. "Luck, that's all." She paused, made a hoarse sob. "Of course, it wasn't so lucky for Cissy."

And the tears started again.

Reed got her another paper towel. If this kept up, he'd need to lend a shoulder as well, but that wouldn't be wise for either of them. Or for Emily, who was still wolfing down the bottle.

"So, if there was nothing…experimental going on at Dearborn," Reed continued, choosing his words, "then maybe there was some other kind of illegal activity. Something that somebody now wants to hide. That brings me back to Cissy and you. Even though Cissy never said so, she might have been coerced into being a surrogate."

That sure didn't help the color in Addison's cheeks. "Coerced? How?"

"I'm still trying to work that out, but there are two possible red flags that are flying pretty high. Your attorney did the surrogacy agreements for both Cissy and her sister, Mellie. Now, on the surface that doesn't seem like such a big thing, but Cissy and Mellie have already been surrogates twice, and they're only in their early twenties."

Addison repeated that "Oh, God." Then, "I didn't know."

"And I'm sure they didn't volunteer the info to you, either. Even if they're *professional* surrogates, the fifty grand you paid Cissy isn't in her bank account. Neither are Mellie's payments. Yeah, they could have spent most of the two hundred thousand that they got in three years, but the problem is that the money's just not showing up anywhere."

"They could have received cash and not deposited any of it in a bank," she suggested.

"True, but there's not even a record of them renting or buying a place. At least not in their own names. The apartment where they live is owned by Dearborn, and Cooper can't even find a record of them paying rent."

She stayed quiet a moment. "So you think someone blackmailed them or forced them into becoming surrogates, and they were being held at that apartment maybe against their will?"

Reed shrugged. "After dealing with the baby farms, anything's possible."

And that brought him to the next red flag.

"Judge Quarles," Reed said. "Both Cissy and her sister were in his program for runaways and high-risk teenagers."

Addison's eyes widened, and he could almost see the thoughts going on in her head. The same ones no doubt that Reed had had when he first learned of the connection. "You think Quarles is part of the baby farms?"

"Could be. Or maybe Quarles started his own version of a baby farm by using troubled teenage girls as surrogates. It wouldn't be hard to get them fake I.D.s so they would appear to be adults."

"Mercy," she said under her breath. Then shook her head. "But why would Quarles have Cissy killed?"

This was the part of his theory that Reed really didn't like. "Maybe Cissy said something about telling someone. Or she could have tried to blackmail him for more money."

"And Quarles could believe that Cissy said something to *me*." She groaned softly. "Cooper has to find out from Mellie what's going on."

That was the plan, but Cooper had said that Mellie sounded past just being nervous on the phone, so maybe the woman wouldn't run before Cooper made it to San Antonio to talk to her. While he was hoping, Reed added that no one would get to Mellie before Cooper did. After all, if her sister had been killed for talking to the wrong person, then Mellie could be in serious danger, too.

"When SAPD checked on Mellie earlier, did they find anything wrong?" Addison asked.

He shook his head. "It was just what we call a welfare check. She answered the door and appeared to be okay. They questioned her briefly about her sister and told her to come in and make an official statement. She said she would, and SAPD left two officers in a patrol car outside her apartment."

Hopefully, that would be enough to deter anyone from going after her. Deter her from running, too.

Emily finished her bottle, and Addison put the baby against her shoulder so she could burp her. At least Reed thought that was what she was doing. Emily, however, used the opportunity to look around.

At Reed.

Those little eyes came right to his, and the corner of her mouth lifted. Another punch to the gut. "I didn't know babies that young could smile."

Addison looked down at the baby and smiled, too. "Amazing, isn't it?"

Yeah. That gave him yet another punch because all of this seemed too cozy. Too natural. And it was anything but. Even if an investigation hadn't been going on, there was still that part about his being sucky father material.

Emily's smile, however, made him feel as if he could do anything.

That made him stupid.

The only thing he needed to be thinking and doing right now was figuring out a way to keep them all safe.

"Some people say it's gas causing them to smile," Addison went on. "But I'm positive it's the real deal."

So was he. And even if it wasn't, that smile was still priceless.

His phone buzzed, and he hoped it wasn't Colt or

Cooper with yet another round of bad news, but the name that popped on the screen wasn't one Reed had been expecting.

"Not Quarles?" Addison asked.

Reed shook his head. "It's the county sheriff, Aiden Braddock."

That put some more concern in Addison's eyes. Aiden wasn't just the son of the man that Jewell was accused of murdering; he was also the sheriff in the county where Jewell was incarcerated.

Before Addison could jump to any bad conclusions, Reed answered the call and put it on speaker.

"Sorry to call so early," Aiden greeted him, "but I thought you'd want to hear this right away. I got a call from the hospital just up the street from my office. A man walked into the E.R. with a gunshot wound to the shoulder."

Reed instantly made the connection. "I shot one of the men who tried to kidnap my ex-wife yesterday."

"Yeah, so the guy said."

"You've talked to him?" Reed couldn't ask fast enough. "And he admitted to attempted kidnapping?"

"I'm with him now," Sheriff Braddock clarified. "And he's admitted to being part of the kidnapping. He said he wants immunity in exchange for information, and he'll give us that information when his lawyer arrives."

Reed wanted to give a shout of relief. This was exactly the kind of break they needed. "How bad is he hurt?"

"Not bad," the sheriff answered. "As soon as the medics are done stitching him up, I'm arresting him and taking him into custody. If you want first crack at him during the interrogation, I suggest you get down here now."

Chapter Eight

Addison prayed this wasn't a huge mistake—leaving Emily with Jewell's daughter Rosalie while Reed and she went to the Clay Ridge County Sheriff's Office to talk with the kidnapper. Reed hadn't wanted her to go at all, but when Addison had insisted, their compromise was to leave the baby at the ranch.

Where Emily would hopefully be safe.

At least she'd be safer there than out on the roads and in the open. At the ranch, there were several lawmen and plenty of armed ranch hands. Maybe that would be enough.

"You can still change your mind," Reed said to her as he pulled into the parking lot of the sheriff's office. "I can call Colt or Cooper to come and get you and take you back to the ranch."

Colt and Cooper were tied up with the investigation and talking with Mellie. Exactly what Addison wanted them to be doing. The lawmen definitely didn't have time to babysit her. Besides, maybe Reed and she would quickly learn the identity of the person who'd hired the kidnappers to come after Emily and her. Once they had a name, then the person could be arrested, and hopefully the danger would end.

"I want to hear what he has to say," Addison insisted,

causing Reed to drag in a long, deep breath. He was probably sick and tired of her. Or at least of the danger that she'd brought with her to Sweetwater Springs.

However, she didn't think that sick and tired applied to Emily.

Addison hadn't missed the way Reed looked at the baby. Like a father looking at his daughter. Soon, very soon, she'd have to make it clear that while Reed could see Emily as part of a custody arrangement, Addison wasn't going to give up the life she'd planned with her precious baby. A life she'd never thought Reed would have wanted any part of anyway.

Reed glanced all around the parking lot before he motioned for her to get out. As they'd done at Cooper's office, they hurried inside. They first had to go through the metal detector, and of course, Reed's gun set it off. The deputy at reception waited until his boss, Sheriff Aiden Braddock, stepped out from an office and gave his wave of approval before he let them in.

It was barely nine in the morning, but the place was already buzzing with activity. Aiden was on the phone, and he held up his finger in a *wait a second* gesture.

There were three other uniformed officers at desks scattered around the room. No sign of the wounded kidnapper, but Addison did spot someone else she knew. Jewell's stepson FBI agent Seth Calder. He was on the phone, too, but put it away when he spotted them.

"What the devil is he doing here?" Reed said under his breath. But he obviously didn't mumble it low enough, because it got Seth's attention.

"I was visiting my mother at the jail," Seth supplied, his voice and expression none too friendly.

Ditto for the glare that Reed aimed at him. Of course,

Addison hadn't expected the two to be on friendly terms: Seth was on Jewell's side and Reed was on Roy's.

"Addison," Seth greeted. "I heard about the trouble you're having. Anything I can do to help?"

It was a generous offer, considering that Seth was working hard to clear his mother's name, but it wasn't an offer that Reed seemed to appreciate.

"She doesn't need help from you," Reed snarled.

Great. Just what she didn't want right now—a man-snarling contest—and she got an even bigger dose of it when Aiden finished his call and strolled toward them. He was a big guy, intimidating not just because of his size but because of his hard eyes and stony expression.

Aiden clearly wasn't in the Jewell camp, because she was accused of murdering his father. Many would say it was a serious conflict of interest for Jewell to be incarcerated in the very county where Aiden was sheriff, but it would have been an even bigger conflict had she been placed in Cooper's custody and the Sweetwater Springs Jail. The alternative would have been to send her farther away, but Jewell's lawyer had apparently managed to nix that.

"I thought you were leaving," Aiden said to Seth.

The two men were about the same size, and Seth looked Aiden straight in the eye. Seth even moved closer, clearly violating Aiden's personal space and then some. "No. I'll leave when I'm ready."

That went over about as well as she'd figured it would. Which was not well at all. Aiden shot both Reed and Seth a look that would have frozen most men in their tracks. Seth gave him back one that could have frozen Hades, and Reed matched it.

Since all this tension was far from helpful, Addison stepped in the middle of the trio. "Thanks for your offer to help, and for giving up the guest cottage for us," she said to Seth in a whisper before turning to Aiden. "Now, may we see the kidnapper?"

Aiden didn't jump to say yes. Seth didn't jump, either. The glares went on for a few moments longer before Seth finally stepped around them and headed for the door. Both Reed and Aiden watched him leave.

"The kidnapper won't give me his name," Aiden explained, leading them down the hall. "And his prints aren't in the system."

That was a surprise. Addison figured the guy would have a record. One look at him when they stepped into the interview room, though, and Addison realized the reason he might not have a record. He was young. He was buff with a marine-like body, but he could still be in his late teens. He was seated in a metal chair with his legs and right hand cuffed to it.

The kidnapper spared them a glance before turning back to stare at the bare wall. "I said I wasn't gonna talk to anybody until my lawyer got here."

"He's on his way," Aiden assured him. "I just figured you'd want to say you're sorry to Mrs. Caldwell here, after you tried to kill her and all."

The guy opened his mouth as if he might jump to deny that, but then he must have remembered that anything he said would be used against him. Of course, he'd already admitted to the kidnapping attempt, so that was the ultimate self-incrimination.

Reed stepped in front of her, walking closer and staring down at the man. "In case you don't know, I'm the man who shot you."

The kidnapper turned back, some anger flashing in his eyes, before he shut down again and merely said, "I know who you are."

Reed stayed quiet a moment, his gaze going from the guy's face to his right arm, which was bandaged and in a sling. "What happened? Did your partners just drop you off at the hospital and leave you?"

He didn't respond to that, not verbally anyway, but his mouth tightened. So, *yes,* that probably was what had happened.

"I'd be riled to the core if they did that to me," Reed went on. "I'd call the sheriff and cut a deal to send those dirtbags to jail. Of course, I'd also want to get the man who hired all of you, since he's the one responsible for this mess you're in."

Addison thought the guy might be fighting back a smile. Maybe he was ready to spill all. "I ain't saying nothing else just yet," he added. "But I'll do a lot of talking to my lawyer when he gets here."

"After that, I expect you to do a lot of talking to us," Reed insisted.

The guy didn't challenge that, but he looked away again, and Aiden tipped his head to the room across the hall. "You two can wait there. I'll let you know when his lawyer shows."

"I don't want you or them listening in when I talk to my lawyer," the guy piped up.

"Wouldn't dream of it," Aiden grumbled.

Aiden had barely shown them into the other interview room when Reed's phone buzzed. This time it was Cooper's name on the screen. Probably because Reed didn't want the kidnapper to hear anything, he shut the door, and instead of putting the call on speaker, he hooked his arm around her and pulled her closer so that she'd be able to listen.

"I'm at Mellie Blanco's place, but she's not here," Cooper said.

Reed groaned. "Wasn't there a patrol watching her?"

"Yeah, and they didn't see her leave. Didn't see anyone come in, either. There are back stairs that lead to a laundry room, and SAPD thinks that's how someone got in or how she got out."

So maybe she hadn't been kidnapped. Still, Addison had to ask, "Are there any signs of an attack? Or worse, murder?"

Cooper paused. "There was some blood on the floor."

Addison's breath vanished and her knees buckled, and if Reed hadn't already taken hold of her, she would have fallen.

"How bad is this?" Reed asked Cooper.

"It's just a few drops in the kitchen, and it could be something as simple as she cut herself. Still, the CSIs will go through the place. I'll let you know what they find. In the meantime, I'm sending Colt to you so he can follow you back when you're finished there."

Addison hated that Colt had to do backup duty. Hated not only that it was necessary but that it was also taking him away from the investigation. Still, with what they'd just learned about Mellie, it could mean the kidnappers were far from finished.

A thought that put a hard knot in her stomach.

The blood on the floor couldn't be a good sign.

"Any chance you can track down the other two babies that Mellie and Cissy carried as surrogates?" Reed asked.

"I can try. Are you thinking those babies might lead us to who's behind this?"

"Maybe." Reed paused a moment. "Maybe stored embryos weren't used for those pregnancies. The babies could have been conceived simply so they could be sold."

True, and if that was what had indeed happened, then the babies' DNA might lead them to the birth fathers.

Or rather the father.

It was a sickening thought that the sisters might have been used as breeding machines, but if they had been, then the babies' DNA could perhaps lead to Cissy's killer.

When he finished his call with Cooper, Reed kept hold of her arm, shoved his phone back in his pocket and then led her to one of the chairs. Addison gladly sat down. For one thing, she still wasn't steady on her feet. For another, it got her out of Reed's grip. His arms were a dangerous place for her to be right now with all this panic racing through her.

"I could have gotten Mellie killed, too," she said, and cursed the tears that came again.

"You didn't get anyone killed." Reed cursed, too, and knelt down in front of her. "Whoever's behind this killed Cissy and maybe hurt her sister, and that idiot across the hall is going to tell us who that person is."

But they might not have stopped the person in time to save two young women. "If it weren't for Cissy, I wouldn't have Emily. The embryo might not have worked in someone else."

Addison figured that was the last thing Reed wanted to discuss, but he made a surprising sound. One of agreement. She looked at him to make sure she hadn't misunderstood.

She hadn't.

Reed's gaze connected with hers, and everything hit her at once. The fear. The adrenaline. Even more of the tears. Addison moved in to drop her head on his shoulder. Something he probably wouldn't like. Instead something else happened that he probably wasn't going to like, either.

He kissed her.

It was just a brush of his mouth on hers. At first. He cursed, snapped away from her as if he'd just made the biggest mistake ever. But the *mistake* got a thousand times worse when the quick kiss turned to something else.

Every muscle in his hands and mouth were rock hard, and she knew he was battling this. A battle he lost because he deepened the kiss.

Oh, mercy.

There it was. The slam of heat she knew only Reed could deliver. Those kisses had seduced her seven years ago when they first started dating, and that was exactly what they were doing now.

His taste slid through her. Firing her up, even though there wasn't much left to fire. Or so she thought, but she'd obviously forgotten that she was being kissed by a man who knew exactly how to make her burn.

He slipped his hand around the back of her neck and hauled her closer. Not that he had to put much effort into it. Addison was already headed that direction anyway, and she landed against his chest with her arms sliding around him.

The kiss had already given her a huge dose of memories. Now the close contact only added to it, and her crazed body clearly thought this was foreplay that would land her in bed with him.

It wouldn't.

First of all, they were in the county sheriff's office, and besides that—there was no way Reed would let this continue.

Addison was right about that, too.

He jerked away from her, and as he'd done in the hospital, Reed moved to the other side of the room. His breath wasn't any steadier than hers, and that was probably why she didn't get an immediate earful of why what they'd just done was wrong and why it wouldn't happen again.

Addison already knew the answer to both.

Reed didn't want another dose of her. Even if their safety hadn't been on the line, it might take a lifetime or two for him to forgive her for not telling him about Emily.

There was a sharp rap at the door. A split second later it opened, and Aiden stuck his head in. "You got a visitor."

"The kidnapper's lawyer," Reed grumbled.

But Aiden shook his head. "It's Judge Quarles."

That brought Addison to her feet. "What does he want?"

"To see you two. Brace yourself. I don't think his mood's very good," Aiden added. "He definitely didn't like having to go through the metal detector."

Welcome to the club. Her mood wasn't good, either, and after what they'd learned about Quarles, he might be responsible for all the bad things that'd been going on.

"Is he armed?" Addison asked.

Aiden shook his head.

"I'll take care of this," Reed said, walking out ahead of her. That was probably his way of telling her to stay put, but despite the fear and Reed's order, Addison wanted a chance to face down the judge.

Reed shot her a scowl from over his shoulder. A totally different look than the one he'd given her before the kisses. However, that had ended in a scowl, too.

Addison followed Aiden and him back into the squad area, and she immediately spotted the man in a charcoal-black suit. Pricey, of course. In fact, everything about

Quarles fell into that category, including his precisely cut blond hair. There was something about him though that surprised her.

Quarles smiled, and he walked to Reed with his hand extended in what appeared to be a friendly greeting. After his somewhat threatening phone call, Addison figured he would lash out at them again. Or rather try. But Reed and she were clearly in lashing-out moods of their own.

"How'd you know Addison and I were here?" Reed demanded.

When Reed didn't shake his hand, Quarles lowered it back to his side, but he kept the demeanor friendly. "I heard about the arrest at the hospital, and I guessed you two would be here to talk to him."

If Reed was buying that, it certainly didn't show on his face.

"So?" Quarles asked, turning to her. "Anything from the kidnapper in custody?"

"He's still waiting on his lawyer," Aiden answered for her. "You're not here to try to talk to him, are you?" He didn't wait for the judge to answer. "Because I can't allow that."

Quarles nodded. "Fair enough. Reed and Addison are actually the ones I came to see. You don't mind if I call you by your first names, do you?"

"I mind," Reed answered. "Now, why don't you tell us about your relationship with the dead woman, Cissy Blanco?"

That caused a quick shift in Quarles's perkiness. His smile vanished. "Perhaps we should take this conversation somewhere more private?"

"You can use the interview room," Aiden offered.

Addison could see Reed's hesitation in his bunched-up forehead. He probably didn't trust Quarles enough to be alone with the man. Still, it wasn't likely that Quarles would attack them in the middle of the sheriff's office, and Aiden had made sure Quarles wasn't armed.

"What about Cissy Blanco?" Reed repeated the moment they were inside the interview room. However, Reed didn't shut the door.

"I was just informed that she and her sister were in one my foundation's programs. I didn't know her, of course. Over the years, there have been hundreds of youngsters in and out of those programs."

It sounded as if Quarles had rehearsed that answer. And he probably had. After all, Reed and she were essentially implicating him in multiple felonies, including murder.

"Are any of the other *youngsters* connected to the baby farms that have been in the news?" Reed asked.

Quarles lifted his shoulder. "I wouldn't know. I don't have any personal connections to the foundation, but there's someone else who does. That's why we need to talk. I can clear up any misconceptions you might have about me while pointing your investigation in the right direction."

"And what direction would that be?" Reed sounded even more skeptical than he looked.

"One where you turn your attention to the guilty party." Quarles reached in his jacket pocket and took out a piece of paper. "That should get you started. There's the proof you need to arrest Addison's attorney, Dominic Harrelson."

Chapter Nine

Reed's first reaction was to curse. "Not again."

First, Rooney had suggested that Quarles might be involved in the baby farms or some other illegal activity. Now it was Quarles's turn to point the finger at someone else.

"Why would my attorney be involved in this?" Addison asked Quarles.

She didn't sound shaken by the judge's accusation, merely riled. Reed was right there with her on that. He had already disliked Quarles because of that earlier phone call, and now Reed's dislike for the man went up a major notch.

"If you don't believe me," Quarles said, the smugness all in his tone and expression, "take a look for yourself." He handed Reed the paper he'd taken from his jacket.

With Addison right by his arm looking on, Reed unfolded the paper, not sure what to expect. There wasn't much, just two names. "Lisa Morretti and Tonya Hanley," Addison read aloud.

Reed looked at her to see if she recognized them, but she only shook her head. "Are we supposed to know who they are?" she challenged Quarles.

"I thought perhaps they'd already come up in your

investigation, especially since they're both missing and were surrogates at Dearborn."

Addison pulled in her breath, making a sharp sound of surprise. "How do you know this?"

"An anonymous source. Someone sent me the names in an email. Don't bother trying to trace the account. My people have already tried, and the sender covered his or her tracks."

Covering up that sort of thing was fairly easy to do if you knew your way around computers, but there was plenty about this that didn't make sense to Reed. "Why send the names to you, and what the heck do those two women have to do with Dominic?"

"I'm still trying to piece this together, but as I said, both women were surrogates at Dearborn, and Dominic was the attorney for both surrogacy arrangements."

Hell. Even if this was a coincidence, Reed figured it was a bad one. Because now there were four surrogates—these two women, Cissy and Mellie—who had connections to the Dearborn Agency and Dominic.

Well, they had connections if Quarles was telling the truth.

Reed wasn't about to trust anything that came out of Quarles's mouth.

He fired off a text to Cooper and asked him to run checks on the two women. If this panned out, then they needed to bring Dominic back in for questioning.

"There's more," Quarles continued when Reed finished his text. "It's obvious that I've been implicated in this unfortunate chain of events, so I've had a few friends doing some research to clear my name. I think there might be a problem with Rooney, the P.I. you hired," he added, looking at Addison.

Oh, man. The bombshells just kept coming, but

before Reed could even respond, the sounds in the hall stopped him.

"The kidnapper's lawyer is here," Aiden let them know. The sheriff opened the door to the room where the kidnapper was waiting, and Aiden ushered in the rail-thin man in a suit.

"Is this the lawyer you wanted?" Aiden asked the kidnapper.

Not a usual question for a suspect, but considering everything that was going on, Reed was glad Aiden had asked it. Better to be safe than sorry. The person who hired the kidnappers could try to sneak someone in to kill the injured man who was hopefully about to tell all.

The kidnapper nodded. "He's my lawyer, Al Crouse."

"Make sure that camera's off," Crouse told Aiden, and he tipped his head to the mirror. "I don't want anybody watching us, either."

"It's off, and you'll have the privacy I'm required to give you." Something that clearly didn't please Aiden, but he shut the door and headed in the direction of his own office.

Maybe it wouldn't be long now before the lawyer could convince his client to accept a deal. One that would trade plenty of information for a reduced sentence. Of course, in this case *reduced* might simply mean taking the death penalty off the table. Often that was enough to get someone to confess.

"Now, back to that accusation about Rooney," Addison said to Quarles. "What kind of *problem* did you mean?"

"Maybe the worst kind. Why exactly did you hire him?"

"To do some background checks." Addison huffed

and folded her arms over her chest. "If Rooney's done something wrong, I need to know."

"When you first met Rooney, did he contact you?" Quarles asked, obviously avoiding Addison's *need to know* comment. "Or was it the other way around?"

Addison stayed quiet a moment. "He contacted me."

And that'd been a red flag for Reed. Well, now after the fact anyway. The P.I. had gone to Addison. Maybe just looking for business.

Or maybe Dearborn and Addison were his business.

"Just tell us what you learned about Rooney," Reed demanded from Quarles.

Quarles's forehead bunched up for a moment. "It's all speculation at this point, but I'm hoping the three of us can get to the truth. In the anonymous email I received, the person claimed Rooney was actually working for the baby farms."

Reed cursed. Addison added some profanity, too, and she dropped down into one of the chairs. Good grief. After everything they'd been through, they darn sure didn't need another suspect.

"What proof did this person have to connect Rooney to the baby farms?" she snapped.

"None that was given to me," Quarles readily admitted, "but there might be something in Rooney's financials to prove a connection. I can help with a court order if necessary."

Normally, Reed wouldn't have been so suspicious of a judge offering help, but this situation was far from normal. "I want a copy of that email," Reed insisted.

Quarles nodded. "I had my secretary print it out. I'll call her and have her courier over a copy. But the email itself won't help resolve any of this. The person only said Rooney was involved and didn't give any details about that involvement." He paused. "I know you and Sheriff McKinnon made some arrests in the baby farms. Did Rooney's name come up at any time?"

"No." Reed didn't hesitate to answer, either, but he played around with that idea for a couple of seconds.

There'd been a lot of covering up with the baby farms. People destroying documents and even the baby farms themselves. Reed wasn't even sure they'd managed to close them all down. Most had been individually run, and while they'd shared some resources, such as doctors, nannies and security guards, there was no central database of information to link them. Or at least nothing that had been discovered yet.

Maybe Quarles's anonymous source would know more about that.

"I'd like to have a better look at your computer, too," Reed insisted.

Quarles certainly didn't jump to agree. "There are files from my foundations on the hard drives. Sensitive information about donations and clients. Wouldn't want that to fall into the wrong hands."

"It won't," Reed promised him. Of course, it was a long shot anyway, but maybe some of that sensitive information would point back to Quarles himself. "I'll make arrangements for someone to pick it up."

After several long moments, Quarles finally made a sound of agreement and then checked his watch. "I have to leave for another appointment. Let me know if you need help with the court order." With that, he turned and walked out.

"Rooney," Addison repeated once Quarles was out of earshot. "You really think he's involved in this?"

"Maybe." And Reed hated that the possibility of his involvement could take this investigation in an even worse direction. "Since Rooney came to you, he might be trying to tie up loose ends with the baby farms. If he works for one of them, that is."

"Loose ends," she repeated, and shuddered. "You mean he could be murdering Dearborn surrogates who may be tied to the baby farms."

Reed settled for a nod. Addison looked as if she could use an arm around her, but this time he stayed back. There was already enough between them without adding more of that.

Addison shook her head. "But why come after me and Emily?"

Too bad Reed had a theory for that, as well. "Rooney could believe that Cissy told you something about the baby farm operation."

"She didn't," Addison said quickly.

And he believed her. That didn't mean Rooney or whoever was behind this believed Addison, though. Any loose end could be dangerous at this point because an arrest in the baby farms' case would also include murder charges. As high profile as this case was, the death penalty would be involved. That meant the stakes were so high the culprit would do anything to cover his tracks.

Reed took out his phone so he could call Cooper and ask him to bring in both Rooney and Dominic for a second round of questioning. However, before he could do that, he heard another sound that grabbed his attention.

A sharp groan.

Followed by a thud.

"The kidnapper," Addison said, already heading in the direction of the other interview room.

Reed stepped in front of her because the kidnapper could have overpowered the lawyer and was maybe trying to use him to escape. He definitely didn't want Addison walking in on that.

"Stay back," Reed warned her.

There was another thud, and Reed drew his gun. So did Aiden when he came running up the hall toward them. Reed got there ahead of him, and he threw open the door of the interview room.

And cursed.

Because both the lawyer and the kidnapper were lying in crumpled heaps on the floor.

SINCE REED AND Aiden were in front of her, it took Addison a moment to see what had caused their alarm.

There was no blood, but both men were lifeless.

"Poison," Reed said immediately.

Addison looked around to see if anyone had gained access through the window, but not only was it shut; it had bars on it. There weren't any vials or telltale signs of poisoning, but someone had certainly done this to them.

"Are they dead?" she asked, pressing her hand to her chest to try and steady her heartbeat.

Reed went to Crouse. Aiden, to the kidnapper. Aiden pressed his fingers to the kidnapper's neck and then shook his head.

Addison sucked in a hard breath and looked at Reed, who was hovering over the lawyer. "He's still alive. Get an ambulance."

Aiden immediately stepped back to make the call, and Addison went closer to Reed. It was hard to be upset at the death of the kidnapper, the very man who'd taken her baby and perhaps also murdered Cissy. But a dead man couldn't give them answers. And judging from the lawyer's shallow breath and icy complexion, he wasn't going to be alive much longer, either.

"What'd you two take?" Reed demanded.

Crouse's eyelids fluttered open for just a moment. "Pills. It'll kill us," he whispered. "It has to kill us."

Obviously, it was doing just that—killing him. "Why did you do this?" Addison asked.

Though his eyes were unfocused, Crouse managed to meet her gaze. "All necessary. I was dying anyway."

And that was all he managed to say. Crouse's breath rattled in his chest, and the life went out of his eyes. Even though Addison didn't have any experience watching someone die, she was certain the lawyer was gone.

Leaving Reed and her with no answers.

"Hell," someone said, and she whipped in the direction of the door to see Colt standing there.

Aiden repeated the profanity. "Crouse was searched before I let him back here," he insisted.

It wouldn't have been hard to conceal pills, especially if Crouse had come here to kill the kidnapper and then commit suicide. There didn't appear to be any signs of a struggle so maybe that meant the kidnapper had cooperated with Crouse's plan.

"But why did this happen?" Addison asked. "If the kidnapper planned on killing himself all along, why come here to do it?"

No one, including Addison, had an answer for that.

"We'll start with Crouse," Reed finally said. "Someone almost certainly hired him to do this."

"I can get his financial records," Colt volunteered.

"And I can push to get an I.D. on the kidnapper," Aiden added. "Once we have that, then maybe we can work out his connection to Crouse and anyone else involved in this."

It was a start, but Addison had to wonder if it'd be enough. The person who'd set this up had no doubt covered his or her tracks. Maybe there wouldn't be any trail, financial or otherwise, to follow.

"I need to get Addison out of here," Reed said, and that was when she realized she was shaking. Something she'd been doing a lot of lately.

She silently cursed her trembling hands and wanted to be stronger, but she was literally looking at two dead men. Plus, she wanted to get back to Emily and make sure she was all right. Addison certainly hadn't forgotten about the danger, but this was a stark reminder of what their attackers were capable of.

"I'll follow you back to the ranch," Colt said, and then he looked at Aiden. "You'll call us as soon as you find out anything?"

Aiden nodded. "Do the same for me."

Colt and Reed assured him that they would, and Reed got her moving toward the front door. However, he didn't let her go out to the parking lot.

"Wait here with Colt," Reed instructed, "and I'll bring the truck around. Someone could be out there watching."

And that someone could be waiting to kill them.

While Reed went for the truck, Colt called Cooper to fill him in on what'd happened, but Addison couldn't hear Cooper's response because of the wail of sirens coming toward the county sheriff's office. Not only was the ambulance too late to save the lawyer or the kidnapper, but the noise was also unnerving because it could mask the sounds of anyone nearby who might be planning on attacking them.

Maybe that had been part of the plan all along—to get them hurrying out of the county sheriff's office. But Reed was obviously taking precautions to make sure another attack didn't happen. As promised, he pulled his truck directly in front of the door so that she only had to take a few steps outside.

"I'll be driving right behind you," Colt said, and hurried to his own truck in the nearby parking lot. Reed didn't pull away until Colt was in his vehicle and ready to go. The ambulance screeched to a stop behind them, and the medics barreled out, heading inside.

As he'd done on the drive over, Reed kept watch around them, but they'd hardly made a few hundred feet from the sheriff's office when his phone buzzed, and Addison saw Cooper's name on the screen. Maybe this wouldn't be yet more bad news.

"I found one of the adoptive parents for the first baby that Mellie gave birth to," Cooper said when Reed answered. "It wasn't a surrogate situation as we originally thought. Mellie got pregnant when she was seventeen, and she gave the baby up. This was a private adoption, one where the adoptive mother paid a considerable sum of money to get the newborn."

Addison felt her pulse jump. "Is the baby okay?" Because things could perhaps go wrong with a private adoption.

"As far as I can tell. I did a quick background check on the adoptive mother. She's single, has a record for embezzling and probably wouldn't have gotten a child through a regular adoption agency. Still, there are no reports that the baby has been harmed in any way. I'll check though to make sure," Cooper added before she could ask.

"Thank you. But what does this mean? And what about the second baby Mellie had?" Addison asked.

"Nothing yet, but we're still looking. It doesn't help that there's no official adoption papers for that particular child."

Addison prayed they would find the child, unharmed. But she also added another prayer—that Mellie and Cissy weren't actually involved in whatever it was that had initiated these attacks.

"If Mellie was part of the baby farm, why wouldn't she have just told someone?" Reed pressed.

"Money, maybe. Or she could have been coerced in some way."

Coerced as in forced to become pregnant. Maybe not by the adoptive parent but by whoever was behind the baby farm.

Like Quarles.

Of course, according to the judge, it could be Rooney or Dominic who'd set up the illegal farms.

"The adoptive mother of Mellie's first child has consented to a DNA test for the baby," Cooper explained. "I'm going to get someone over there with a kit today." He paused. "Are you two okay?"

Reed opened his mouth, maybe to confirm that they were, but his attention went to the side mirror. Addison looked behind them and saw a black car had cut Colt off. Just like that, her thoughts jerked back to all those bad memories of Emily's kidnapping and the aftermath. God, this couldn't be happening again.

"It could be nothing," Reed said as if trying to convince her. And himself. "Cooper, I'll call you back," he added, and ended the call so he could no doubt focus all his attention on the black car.

"I only see one person inside," Addison said to him.

Reed nodded and kept volleying his attention between the car and their surroundings. Since this was the main street that led to the hospital and a shopping area, there was a steady flow of traffic both ahead of and behind them. All normal. Except after everything that'd happened, nothing about this felt normal.

Addison was so focused on the car that when she heard the loud banging sound, it took her a moment to realize what had happened.

And it wasn't good.

A huge truck had come from a side road and had plowed right into the passenger's side of Colt's vehicle. Of course, that brought Colt to a stop. However, that wasn't all Addison saw.

"He's got a gun!" Reed said, taking the words right out of her mouth.

Addison caught just a glimpse of the driver of the black car.

And the gun that he lifted toward Reed and her.

Chapter Ten

Reed couldn't risk stopping to make sure Colt was okay. Especially because that particular collision had likely been designed to prevent Colt from being able to help Addison and him and give them much-needed backup.

If so, it'd worked.

Colt was at a standstill, and the driver of the black car looked ready to kill them.

"Hold on," Reed told Addison a split second before he gave his steering wheel a sharp turn to the left.

There was no one else on the side road, thank goodness, because Reed took the turn way too fast and had to fight to keep control of his truck. Still, that was better than being shot, and it got them out of the immediate line of fire.

But they weren't out of the woods yet.

The black car made the same turn and raced right back toward them. It wouldn't be long before the driver got himself in a position to take aim at them again.

"Call Cooper," Reed said, tossing Addison his phone. He also drew his gun. "Tell him what happened and that we might need backup."

In this case, backup would have to come from the nearby county sheriff's office. Something that Aiden wasn't going to like, since he had his hands full with two dead bodies. But there wasn't much of a choice. Colt could be especially at risk, as he was a sitting duck. At least Reed could try to get away from this idiot.

Addison's voice was shaking, but she made the call while Reed tried to put some distance between them and the black car. Not easy to do. The driver just sped up until he was right on Reed's bumper.

"Cooper said he'd get someone out to help Colt and us ASAP," Addison relayed when she finished her call. "He can track us both through your phones."

Good. Reed knew that Cooper could do that. The phones were issued through the sheriff's office, but that still didn't mean someone could reach Colt or them in time to stop another attack.

"I don't recognize the guy behind us, do you?" Addison asked a moment later.

That was when Reed realized she was peering into the side mirror. She was way too high in the seat, so Reed pushed her right back down.

"No, I don't recognize him."

But he was almost certainly connected to the earlier kidnapping attempt. Maybe the baby farms, too. If so, the driver had likely been sent there to kill Addison.

Reed had to make sure that didn't happen.

A shot blasted into the back of his truck. Reed heard the metal pinging sound when it bounced off the tailgate. Maybe the bullet had ricocheted and hit an innocent bystander. There wasn't anyone else on the road, but there were nearby buildings, and someone could be inside.

Reed's instincts were to get the shooter far away from town and all the civilians, but that probably wouldn't be the safest thing for Addison. If their attacker managed to stop them the way Colt had been stopped, then Addison would almost certainly be killed.

Another shot came at them, this one blasting into his side mirror. Obviously, the guy was having trouble shooting from a moving car, but Reed couldn't risk him getting lucky.

Reed took another sharp turn down a narrow side street. Then another. He cursed when he saw the sign for the elementary school just ahead. He wasn't familiar with this area of Clay Ridge, but the last he wanted to do was endanger any children.

And that led him to a really bad thought.

"Call Cooper again," he told Addison, and he made a turn, one that would take him in the opposite direction of the school. "Make sure everything's okay at the ranch."

As expected, that caused the color to drain from Addison's face, and she jabbed the call button so hard that Reed was surprised the phone didn't break. He wanted to assure her the call was just a precaution, but they might be well past the precaution stage. With Colt's *accident* this could be a three-pronged attack meant not only to take out Addison but to get Emily, as well.

"My baby," Addison managed to say the moment Cooper answered. "Is she all right?"

Reed couldn't hear Cooper's response, and he couldn't take his attention off the driver of that black car. Especially when the guy stuck his arm outside the window again and fired another shot. This one missed the truck completely, but the next one crashed into the rear window. The safety glass sprayed everywhere, but thankfully the shards missed both Addison and him.

Reed could no longer see out the back, but he had no trouble spotting the green SUV on a side road. However, he flew by it so fast that he didn't get a glimpse of who was inside.

"Oh, God," Addison said at the end of a gasp.

Reed's heart practically jumped out of his chest. "Is something wrong with Emily?"

Addison shook her head and pressed the end call button on the phone. "Cooper said all was well at the ranch." She pointed back to a side road that they'd just passed. "I gasped because I think Rooney was in that SUV we just passed."

Rooney?

What the heck was he doing here in Clay Ridge?

Rooney had said he was staying at a hotel in Sweetwater Springs, so maybe he'd followed Addison and him to the county sheriff's office.

Reed glanced in his rearview mirror and got another look at the dark green SUV that was there. Maybe parked or maybe waiting to pull out onto the main road where Reed and their attacker were.

It didn't take long for Reed to get an answer.

The SUV screeched out from the side road and was headed in their direction.

Mercy.

Reed hoped Rooney wasn't about to start shooting at them, too. One attacker was more than enough with Addison in the truck with him.

He pushed the accelerator even harder, putting some distance between them and the school. Between them and the town, as well.

Reed prayed there wouldn't be any trouble with Cooper tracking them. Of course, by now someone had no doubt noticed the shooter, had probably even reported the gunfire, but since Reed couldn't stay in one place, it could still take some time for Cooper or Aiden to catch up with them.

"Hold on," he warned Addison right before he took another sharp turn onto another road.

The driver of the black car fired two more shots, both of them slamming into the truck. And worse.

One went into the tire.

The steering wheel jerked to the right, making it next to impossible for Reed to keep control of the truck.

"Get the gun out of the glove compartment," he told Addison.

She nodded and grappled with the handle of the glove compartment. Her breathing was way too fast, and there wasn't much color left in her cheeks, but she managed to get the gun out. He hated that once again she was in a position where she might have to defend herself, but Reed didn't have a lot of options here.

From what he could tell, there was only one person in the car, and he could no longer see Rooney's SUV. Even if Rooney was planning to get in on this attack, Reed figured his odds were better when it came to facing down the two of them rather than continuing to try and outrun them with a flat tire.

Plus, Reed would have a much harder time returning fire while he was driving, and no way did he want Addison trying to do that.

Because he had no choice, Reed slowed down, ready to pull off the side of the road, but the car only sped up and rammed into them. The jolt was instant, and even though Addison and he were wearing seat belts, it slung them both forward.

Reed barely managed to hang on to his gun, and Addison's went flying. She reached down to get it just as the car rammed into them again.

Hell.

Addison's head smacked against the dashboard, and she tried to bite back a sound of pain. She didn't quite manage it, but she was able to pick up the gun.

Just as the driver hit them for a third time.

Obviously, the car's front bumper was reinforced in some kind of way. It wasn't crumpling from the double impact. Nor had the driver's airbag deployed. That likely meant this had been part of their attacker's plan.

And Reed suddenly figured out what that plan was.

Their truck was being forced into a deep and muddy ditch. Once that happened, Addison and he would be unable to move. That would make them much easier pickings for the gunman. Then, if he wanted to try to take Addison alive, he could. That didn't mean Reed was going to let this dirtbag succeed.

The car rammed into them again. Then again.

Reed fought to keep the truck out of the ditch, and he pushed the button to lower the window. He took aim at the car as best he could and fired. The bullet hit the front windshield, but it didn't shatter.

Bulletproof glass.

Yeah, this wasn't an ordinary car. It'd no doubt been designed to make it easier for the gunman to launch this attack while keeping himself protected.

Reed threw the truck into gear, and even though the flat tire didn't give him much traction, he somehow managed to get them back on the road.

For a few seconds anyway.

Then the car came at them again. And again.

Reed had to choice but to gun the engine and try to get away. Not that he could do that too fast because of the tire, but maybe he could buy a little time so backup could arrive.

"Rooney," Addison said. Again, she was looking out her side window.

Reed glanced behind them, too, and spotted the SUV making its way up the road toward them. He wasn't sure if Rooney was there to help or join the attack so Reed kept to his plan of trying to get them out of there.

The flat tire slapped on the asphalt, and it didn't take long for the tire rim to cut through the rubber. Reed kept on moving. But so did the car and Rooney. However, the car didn't ram into them again. Like an animal waiting to pounce, it just continued to follow them, dropping back in speed as Reed was forced to do.

Reed's phone buzzed, and Addison snatched it up. "It's Rooney."

This definitely wasn't the time for a conversation, but Reed did want to know why the P.I. was out there. "Answer it."

However, Reed tried not to let the call distract him. He kept driving. Kept watch of both the car and the SUV.

"I can help," Rooney blurted out the moment Addison put the call on speaker.

Reed wasn't sure he could trust Rooney's idea of help. "Who's the guy in the car?" he asked Rooney.

"I don't know. I got a call from a criminal informant who said there was going to be trouble in Clay Ridge. I drove here to check it out."

And Rooney just happened to be on the same road with them at the time of the attack? The timing was certainly suspicious, but then maybe Quarles or Dominic had wanted to make Rooney look guilty so they could throw suspicion off themselves. If so, they could have staged a call from a criminal informant, since it was easy enough to pay one of them off to do something like this.

"What do you want me to do?" Rooney asked Reed.

"Try to distract the guy after us."

He wasn't sure how Rooney would do that—or if he would attempt anything that would actually help—but Reed was a little surprised when Rooney rammed his SUV into the back of the car. Maybe the rear bumper wasn't reinforced like the front, because the impact definitely gave the gunman's car a jolt.

Good.

It might only be a small temporary distraction, but at this point Reed would take what he could get.

Rooney rammed into the car again, and even over the sound of the bumpers colliding, Reed heard something he definitely wanted to hear.

A siren.

Help was on the way.

Rooney rammed into the car for a third time, and Reed got a glimpse of the driver's face. The dirtbag was smiling as if this was some kind of adventure.

Or maybe just part of some sick plan that Rooney and he had devised.

The tire rim of Reed's truck continued to scrape against the pavement, and the black smoke started to billow up in front of them. It didn't take long for the stench of burning rubber to pour through the truck's cab and cause both Addison and him to start coughing.

Worse, Reed could no longer see the road surface in front of them. "I have to stop."

That didn't help Addison's uneven breathing, and she raised her gun, ready for the next wave of attack.

But it didn't come.

The driver of the car jerked the steering wheel to

his left and hit the accelerator. He sped around Reed's truck and kept going.

So did Rooney.

"He's getting away!" Reed heard Rooney shout through the phone.

And Rooney took off after the man.

Chapter Eleven

"Rooney's still not answering his phone," Reed said.

Addison figured that wasn't a good sign. It'd been over an hour since Rooney drove off after the gunman who'd attacked them. If Rooney had managed to catch up with the guy, he would almost certainly have called Reed to let him know. That hadn't happened. So it could mean the gunman had taken out Rooney.

Yet someone else could be dead because of her.

Reed answered one more phone call, his attention still nailed to her. It was pretty much where his attention had been after they arrived back at the sheriff's office. He was probably checking to make sure she wasn't falling apart.

And that would happen.

Addison was sure of it.

She just didn't want to break down in front of Cooper, Colt and Reed. Not when they had much more important things to do than watch her shatter into a thousand little pieces. Reed, Colt and she had come way too close to dying again, and the more time the lawmen could devote to the investigation, the sooner they might be able to make an arrest and stop the danger.

It had to stop.

Especially for Emily's sake.

"We got the DNA test done on the first baby Mellie had," Cooper said when he finished his latest call.

Addison had no idea how long it would take to get a possible match on the baby's father, but maybe it would pan out and give them some info about the case. Well, it would if the baby's father was connected to the baby farms and any other illegal activity going on. Maybe it wasn't anything nearly as sinister as that, and perhaps Mellie had gotten pregnant by her boyfriend. However, they couldn't ask the woman about that until they found her.

Ditto for Rooney. They wouldn't know if he'd learned anything about the gunman unless he contacted them, and since he wasn't answering his phone, Addison had no idea how long it'd be before they heard from him.

If ever.

"There's more," Cooper said, his attention shifting to Addison.

Oh, no. The sheriff had *that* look. The one that told her he was about to deliver another dose of bad news.

"When the cops were going through Mellie's apartment," Cooper continued, "they found a letter that Cissy wrote to you. Did Cissy ever mention anything about writing to you?"

Addison had to shake her head. "No. If Cissy wanted to tell me something, why didn't she just call or text me? She had my phone number."

"I'm not sure. SAPD will fax us a copy of the letter, but it appears to be some kind of warning."

That gave her another punch of fear she didn't need. Addison was all too aware of the danger, but maybe there'd be clues in the letter that would help the investigation. Maybe.

"What exactly did the letter say?" she asked Cooper.

"The detective didn't want to read it aloud to me. He was at Mellie's apartment, and the landlord was still there. He wasn't sure if the guy was in on Mellie's disappearance or not and figured he'd better be safe. He said it won't take them long to fax it. He's headed back to his office now."

Any length of time was too long to wait. Of course, if the letter wasn't meant to be of any help to them, then Addison wasn't sure her frayed nerves could deal with just another threat. There'd already been too many of those.

Reed finished his call, too, and he walked over to where she was seated next to his desk. "I made arrangements for a safe house for Emily and you. It should be ready within an hour or so, and I can take you two there."

A safe house was exactly what Emily needed. At least, it would be better than the arrangement they had now. Rosalie and the rest of the McKinnons had generously agreed to keep the baby at the Sweetwater Ranch, but that put them all in danger. Still, a safe house wasn't the only thing they could do to protect Emily.

"We got a problem," Colt said before Addison could bring up her concerns about the safe house to Reed. "I just got off the phone with a criminal informant who told me that Rooney hired some muscle and a triggerman just a few days ago."

Addison could have sworn her stomach dropped to her knees. "A criminal informant? Can the guy be trusted?"

"According to the San Antonio cops, this one can be."

That caused Reed to curse. "Any chance hiring them was just part of Rooney's investigation? Maybe he was actually trying to make contact with someone involved in the baby farm?"

Colt shook his head. "As far as I can tell, the thugs he hired don't have a connection to the baby farm. But they might have a connection to the dead kidnapper at the county sheriff's office. One of the thugs, Timmy Marcellus, matches the description of our dead guy to a tee."

Reed repeated the name as if trying to see if he recognized it. "But our dead guy's prints weren't in the system."

"And neither are Marcellus's. He's been evading arrest for several years now. Anyway, the county sheriff sent the criminal informant a photo of our dead guy, and the CI made a positive I.D."

At least they now had a name for the dead kidnapper. A name they'd hoped to use to track down the person who'd hired him. But that person might be Rooney, someone she'd hired. And had trusted.

"Why would Rooney go after the gunman if he's the one behind the attacks?" she asked.

The three lawmen exchanged glances, but it was Reed who answered, "Maybe he didn't *go after* him. Maybe he wanted to make sure the guy got away."

And if that was true, it had likely worked. After all, no one had spotted their attacker or Rooney since they'd fled the scene.

"What about the dead lawyer?" Addison continued. "Is he connected to Rooney, too?"

"I'm still working on that," Colt said. "The lawyer, Al Crouse, was dying. Cancer. He had only a couple of months to live. So he could have agreed to a murder-suicide pact if someone was giving his family a lot of money."

Because her head was whirling with this new information, it took Addison a moment to sort through it all. "But why would Marcellus call Crouse to come to the sheriff's office if he suspected the lawyer might try to kill him?"

Colt just lifted his shoulder. "Perhaps Marcellus thought Crouse would help him. Or maybe Marcellus knew he was a dead man, that his boss was going to kill him in a much more painful way, so he called in Crouse to do the job."

And by doing *the job,* it prevented the cops from getting information that could stop this danger.

"That's why I need to move Emily and you to a safe house," Reed added. "The person behind this is willing to do anything to conceal his or her identity."

Addison believed that with all her heart, and that was why she had to do something she truly didn't want to do.

"The kidnappers are after *me,*" she reminded Reed. "If I go to the safe house with Emily, they'll try to find me. And if they do, they'll find her, too."

Reed was shaking his head before she even finished. "We'll have to take lots of precautions. We'll have to make sure these snakes don't find the location of the safe house."

"But what if they do?" she asked but didn't wait for an answer. "They could find it, and Emily could be hurt." Or worse. "I don't want to take that risk."

Reed huffed, stared at her. "What are you saying?"

"That I want Emily to go to the safe house with all the protection you can get for her. I'll stay here in Sweetwater Springs. That way, the kidnappers will come after me and stay away from her."

That got Reed cursing. "You're talking about using yourself as bait. That's not gonna happen."

"You'd rather Emily be in danger?" she argued.

Reed's cursing continued. "I want you both safe." He opened his mouth, as if to add more, but he ended up just repeating himself in a tone filled more with frustration than anger.

A tone that Addison herself was feeling.

"I want that, too," she said. "And I want you and all the McKinnons safe, as well. That can't happen with me around. Anywhere I go, the danger will just follow. You said yourself this person will do anything to conceal his identity." Addison had to clear her throat to continue. "He won't stop, and you know that."

"We could do two safe houses," Colt offered just as Reed looked ready to launch into another round of profanity. "In fact, other than Addison and you being away from Emily, it might be easier to have two."

Reed gave Colt a look that could have withered fresh spring grass. "Whose side are you on?"

"The side of catching the dirtbag trying to get to Addison. Think it through, Reed. If we bring in a witness or some other person of interest, you and Addison are going to want to be here to listen in on the interview. Going back and forth between the safe house with Emily only increases the chances that someone could find the location."

Colt was right, and judging from the groan Reed made, he knew Colt was right, too. Still, he apparently wasn't ready to admit that, because he opened his mouth, closed it and then cursed again.

"You'll be away from Emily," Reed reminded her. "Have you thought of that, huh?"

Yes, and it sickened her to think of not being with her precious baby. Still, it sickened her more to think of the danger breathing down their necks.

"Maybe I won't have to be away from her for long,"

Addison said. "With her safe, then I can focus on finding the person who wants me dead."

That sent Reed's jaw muscles stirring again. Maybe because he didn't like this idea or maybe because she said *I* and not *we.* Either way, she braced herself for more of Reed's argument, but the whirring sound of the fax machine cut off anything else he was about to say.

Colt went to the fax machine and picked up the first page that came out. "It's the letter Cissy wrote to Addison." He glanced through it and handed it to her.

Addison was almost afraid of what Cissy had written, and she didn't read it alone. Reed went to one side. Cooper, the other. Both were obviously interested in what the dead surrogate had to say. The letter was a single page and handwritten in an almost childlike scrawl.

"Addison," she read aloud, "I can't risk calling you. I think they've bugged my phone, so I'm going to see if I can get this letter to you somehow. I'm real sorry. I opened a can of worms, and now I maybe got us both in trouble. I remember you talking about your ex, saying he was a cop of some kind. You should go to him and see if he'll help keep you and Emily safe..."

Cissy had indeed done something that'd maybe set all this in motion. But what? And who were the *they* who'd possibly tapped her phone?

"I can't do anything now to make this stop," Addison read on, "but I need your ex to do me a big favor. Have him find Violet Martin, the baby I gave up for adoption. Make sure she doesn't get hurt. This is big. Bigger than I even thought in the beginning. I don't have the proof, but I know he's the one behind all these baby farms."

Addison finished reading the letter and looked at Colt. *"He?"* she repeated. She looked through the letter again, hoping that Cissy had clarified who *he* was.

But the woman hadn't.

However, Cissy had made several other things crystal clear. Like the danger. Not just to Emily, Reed and her, but to the other child, as well.

"Has anything come up about this baby, Violet?" she asked.

Colt shook his head. Cooper and Reed did the same. However, both Cooper and Colt hurried to their computers to start checking.

"The records at Dearborn are missing," Reed reminded her. "But there could be an adoption record for the baby. If there is, we'll find her."

Reed looped his arm around her waist and got her moving in the direction of his desk. He had her sit in the chair across from his and passed her a bottle of water that he took from a small fridge behind him.

"If Cissy knew she was in danger," Addison said to Reed, "why didn't she just go to the cops?"

"Maybe because she didn't trust them. How much do you know about her life before she became your surrogate? *Our* surrogate," he corrected in a mumble under his breath.

There it was again. The big elephant in the room. Along with the attraction still simmering between them, it only complicated this situation even more.

"I know only what I've already told you," Addison insisted. "Truth is, I didn't want to know more about her. Yes, at the time I was beyond happy that she was able to carry Emily, but Cissy was also a reminder of what I desperately wanted to do myself, but couldn't."

Something Addison had risked her life to do. And that was yet something else between Reed and her.

"Now let's talk about this safe house and Emily," he said. She braced herself for the continued argument, but Reed only sighed. "You're sure you want a separate safe house for Emily?"

Addison didn't trust her voice, and she nodded. It nearly crushed her to think of leaving her baby even for a short while, but she believed with all her heart that it was necessary.

Reed gave another of those weary sighs and took out his phone to start the preparations for the second house. However, he'd barely gotten started with it when Colt spoke.

"I found something on Cissy's baby," Colt said.

That seemed way too fast for Addison, and she prayed he hadn't found her because the baby had been kidnapped or harmed.

"When we were looking for Mellie's baby, I got access to statewide adoption records," Colt went on. "And I just now looked through those again and found Violet. It was a private adoption, and her adoptive parents moved to Florida several months ago. No phone number contact, but I can have the local police do a welfare check."

"Please, do that." Addison couldn't say it fast enough. But it made her wonder—had the baby's adoptive parents moved because they'd been aware of the possible danger?

"Anything irregular about Violet's adoption?" Reed asked.

"Maybe. Like the adoptive mother for Mellie's baby, this woman has a record for a white-collar crime. Nothing to especially indicate that she'd be a bad parent, but I doubt she would have been able to adopt using the conventional route."

And that brought them right back to Dearborn again.

She hated how everything seemed to be *irregular*

there. Her first clue should have been when Cissy was given the amino test because of a possible mix-up with the embryos. But at that point Addison hadn't wanted to see beyond her own happiness—that she was within months of becoming a mother.

"If Mellie and Cissy were more than just birth mothers," Reed said, "if they were intentionally impregnated so their babies could be sold, then the babies' DNA might tell us who's behind the illegal operation at Dearborn."

Yes, and that meant the babies could be in danger. Maybe the kidnappers wouldn't harm the children, but they could remove them from their families and maybe send them out of the country so they wouldn't essentially become evidence against the monster who'd put all this into action.

But something about that didn't make sense, either.

"There was nothing shady about my surrogacy arrangement with Cissy," she reminded him. "I hired her, paid her and she handed over the baby that she carried for me."

Reed nodded. "I suspect when we unravel this Dearborn mess, we'll find other surrogacy arrangements that weren't forced or weren't part of the baby farms. Dearborn would need something legitimate on their books. Records that wouldn't point to any illegal activity."

True. And Dearborn did make some money from the surrogacy deal with Cissy.

"If the person behind this hadn't thought Cissy had spilled something to you," Reed went on, "then I don't believe the kidnappers would have come after you."

Addison had to agree with that, as well. "Maybe the kidnappers knew Cissy had written that letter to me.

Cissy thought someone was listening in on her conversations, but maybe they had her apartment bugged, too."

All three voiced some kind of agreement with that. It didn't help her stomach, which was knotted and churning, because it only verified the reason for the danger. And it certainly didn't put an end to it.

"No," Reed said, bringing her attention back to him. "Please tell me you're not thinking about trying to ditch me in order to keep me out of the path of those kidnappers."

Since that was exactly what she was thinking, Addison hiked up her chin and tried to look a lot stronger than she felt. Hard to do when everything inside her was spiraling with fear and worry.

"SAPD could take over my protection detail. You could go to the safe house with Emily. At least consider it," she said before he could flat-out refuse.

Judging from the way Reed's forehead bunched up, he had no intention of considering her plan, so Addison was about to play the baby card. She could remind him that Emily's safety had to come first. Above hers. And even above Reed's own concerns about how his fatherhood had come about. That meant Reed should be part of Emily's protection detail. However, Addison didn't get a chance even to start that particular argument.

Because the door flew open.

Colt, Cooper and Reed all turned in that direction, all of them drawing their guns. In the same motion, Reed hooked his left arm around her and pulled her behind him. With good reason.

It was Rooney who came through the door.

Chapter Twelve

Reed's body geared up for a fight with the man they now considered a top suspect.

Rooney.

But Reed quickly realized that this might not be a fighting situation when he saw the blood on Rooney's shirt. The P.I. wasn't armed, either. His face was practically colorless, and he dropped to his knees.

"Call an ambulance," Cooper told Colt before he and Reed went to Rooney.

However, Reed motioned for Addison to stay back. Yes, it appeared the P.I. was injured, but he didn't want to take the chance that this might be a ruse so the kidnappers could have another go at taking her.

"What happened to you?" Cooper asked the man.

Rooney clutched his hand to his bleeding shoulder. "The kidnapper shot me. I managed to get away from him and drove back here."

"Here?" Reed repeated. "You should have gone straight to the hospital or called an ambulance."

And that made Reed even more suspicious of Rooney's behavior. He checked outside to make sure they weren't about to be attacked. He couldn't see anyone, but just in case, he motioned for Addison to go back into the hall.

"The ambulance is on its way," Colt informed them. "I also called in Pete so he can ride with Rooney to the hospital."

Good idea. Pete was usually the night deputy, and while he wouldn't be happy about being called in, Reed wanted the P.I. to have a police escort. Ditto for Addison's move to the safe house, and Reed figured Colt and he would do that while Cooper manned the office.

Colt, too, joined Reed and Cooper at the front. Like Reed, Colt kept his gun drawn, ready in case things turned worse than they already were.

Reed stooped lower so he could get right in Rooney's face. "Tell me about the thugs you hired to come after Addison and the baby."

Rooney's eyes widened, and he shook his head. "I didn't hire any thugs. And I especially didn't hire anybody to come after Addison. Who the hell said I did?"

"A reliable source." Reed hoped. Still, he wanted more than just the word of a CI before he arrested Rooney.

The fact that Rooney had been shot made Reed think the man could be innocent. Or he was being set up. Of course, Rooney could have arranged to be shot so it'd throw suspicion off himself, especially after the accusations against him.

"I hired two people, not thugs," Rooney admitted. "They were to track down information about Dearborn and the baby farms. I damn sure didn't tell them to hurt or kidnap anyone."

Cooper and Reed exchanged glances. It was hard to tell if Rooney was lying. "I want the names of the men you hired."

He nodded and, grimacing again, Rooney reached into his pocket. That got Cooper and Reed pointing their guns at him. "I'm just getting my phone," the P.I. snarled.

Rooney handed the phone to Cooper. "Their names and contact info are in the recent calls. The ones before I phoned Reed during the attack."

Cooper scrolled through the recent calls and spotted the two names. Not Marcellus's name, but he could be using an alias. Colt took the phone and got started.

"Did you get a good look at the kidnapper who shot you?" Reed asked.

Rooney shook his head. "But I got the license plate numbers." And he rattled them off. However, Reed had already made note of them and phoned them in.

"The plates were fake," Reed explained.

Just as he'd expected they would be. No way would the person responsible for the attack have allowed those plates to be traced back to him or her.

"I think I bit off more than I could chew with this investigation." Rooney grimaced in pain, and even though Addison was all the way at the back of the squad room, the P.I. looked in her direction. "I swear I didn't know it'd come to this when I started looking around."

Maybe not. But that reminded Reed of something he'd wanted to ask the P.I. "Why exactly were you looking around in the first place, and what's the name of the CI who told you about the possible trouble out in Clay Ridge?"

Rooney pulled in a long breath and dragged his tongue over his bottom lip. "The CI is a guy called Speed who lives on the Riverwalk. Not sure what his real name is, but SAPD uses him, so they might know."

"I'll call them about that, too," Colt volunteered.

It might have been his imagination playing tricks on him, but that seemed to unnerve Rooney a little. Maybe because the P.I. was lying? If the CI didn't pan out, then that wouldn't play well in Rooney's favor.

"And the investigation?" Reed pressed. "Why'd you even start it?"

"I already told you. There were irregularities at Dearborn, and I wanted to make sure they weren't involved with the baby farms."

There was still something about that reason that didn't sound right, but Reed didn't get a chance to push Rooney for more answers, because the ambulance came to a stop in front of the sheriff's office. Soon, though, once the doctors checked out Rooney, Reed wanted to question him further. In the meantime, maybe those calls that Colt was making would pan out.

Pete pulled up right behind the ambulance. Thank goodness, he lived in town and had come right in.

"One of us will come to the hospital so we can finish this talk," Reed said to Rooney.

He nodded as if looking forward to it. "Good. Because I want to get this dirtbag who tried to kill me."

Reed wanted the same thing. And fast.

He stood and watched as the medics put Rooney in the ambulance. Pete got in as well, and once the ambulance drove away, Reed turned to make sure Addison was okay.

And he could have sworn his heart missed a beat or two.

Because she wasn't there.

Reed practically ran into Cooper, maneuvering him aside while he hurried to the hall where he'd last seen her. After everything that'd happened, plenty of bad things went through his head. *Plenty.* But when he heard the water running in the bathroom, he realized that he'd let his imagination get the best of him.

The bathroom door was open, and Addison was at the sink. She turned toward him, the water sliding from her face and onto the front of her shirt. Her mouth was trembling. The worry was there in her eyes. All over her actually.

Even with the fear, the moment caught him off guard, and he felt the old fire between them. It slid through him and for that brief moment, all the bad blood washed away.

The memories came. Damn them. Memories of other times that her beautiful face had caused a frenzy inside him. Other times when she'd been his for the taking.

Unlike now.

And then he saw the tears.

Reed got to her as fast as he could, and despite the warning that his head was giving him to stay back, he pulled her into his arms.

"I'm not going to cry," she assured him. "You have enough to deal with."

Yeah, he did. But he could add one more thing. Especially when that one thing was Addison. Reed pulled her even closer.

"I brought Rooney into this," she said, her voice a shaky whisper. "I should never have hired him."

"If you hadn't and he's behind the kidnapping attempts, he would have just found another way to put himself in this investigation."

Judging from the huff she made, Addison didn't believe a word he was saying.

Reed cupped her chin, forcing eye contact so that she could see he wasn't just giving her lip service. But another look at her, and he felt that punch again.

The one he darn sure shouldn't be feeling right about now.

Not with them so close and her mouth just a few inches from his.

A part of him—definitely not his brain—reminded him that a kiss wouldn't be such a bad thing right now. Their nerves were raw and frayed. Emotions, sky-high. And a kiss might be the ticket to settling them both down.

It was a bad lie, of course.

But Reed's body just went along with it, and he lowered his head and kissed her.

If he thought he got an avalanche of memories before, that was nothing compared to what he got now. This wasn't one of those little pecks of reassurance. The heat went bone-deep, and it silenced any part of him that was trying to stay logical and keep away from her.

There was nothing logical about this.

At least the kiss dried up Addison's tears. She took hold of his forearms, dragging him closer and kissing him right back.

That made them both stupid.

But even stupidity didn't stop them. Nope. Reed just kept on kissing her. Kept on pulling her closer and closer even though the only way closer could happen was for the clothes to go.

Thank goodness things didn't get that far. But he had to wonder just what would have stopped them if they'd been somewhere private and not in the restroom of the sheriff's office.

The sound of footsteps had them flying apart. In the nick of time, too. Because Cooper appeared in the doorway. Of course, Cooper no doubt knew what was going on, but he only gave Reed a raised eyebrow.

Considering the hell Reed had gone through with the divorce—hell that Cooper had experienced right along with him—a raised eyebrow wasn't much of a criticism. Still, it was enough to remind Reed that he wasn't just playing with fire. He was playing with Addison's heart.

And his own.

"Are you two…okay?" Cooper asked. Though Reed figured his longtime friend and boss really wanted to use the word *crazy* instead of *okay.*

"We're fine," Addison answered, and Reed managed something along the same lines.

Cooper nodded, clearly not believing them, but he didn't press the issue. "Colt's checking into those men Rooney hired, but we just got another call from the lab. It's about the DNA results."

"For Mellie's baby?" Reed asked.

Cooper shook his head. "For Emily."

Oh, man. That came at him like another punch, and Reed pulled in his breath. Held it. Waited.

"She's yours and Addison's," Cooper explained.

Addison released a breath of relief, too. Though Emily's paternity had never been in question. Not in their minds anyway. Still, it was good to have it confirmed with DNA. With all the shady things going on at Dearborn, at least they hadn't messed up the in vitro procedure.

"Now, are you okay?" Cooper repeated, his attention on Reed.

Reed knew what Cooper was really asking—could he handle fatherhood? Cooper was a father of one himself and had another on the way so he knew this couldn't be a half-assed commitment on Reed's part. And it didn't matter Addison had gone behind his back to have this child. The only thing that mattered now was that Emily got the father she deserved.

Too bad Reed wasn't sure he could be that kind of dad.

Though he'd do whatever it took to keep her safe. To do what was best for her. To love her.

"I'm okay," Reed answered, and he hoped that was the truth.

"We got visitors," Colt called out.

Just like that, the emotion vanished. Well, that particular emotion anyway, and it was replaced by a healthy dose of concern. Especially since the murdering kidnapper was still at large.

"Stay behind me," Reed warned Addison.

Reed stepped into the hall with Cooper, and he spotted Dominic as he opened the front door. And he wasn't alone. There was a tall, dark-haired man with the lawyer. Because Dominic was a suspect and the other guy was a stranger, Reed drew his gun again.

Dominic opened his mouth to say something, but the blood on the floor must have caught his attention. "What the heck happened here?"

"Rooney was injured," Colt answered. He slid his hand over his gun. "The ambulance took him to the hospital."

"Oh, God," Dominic said, looking very concerned for a man who'd tossed some serious accusations at Rooney. He frantically shook his head. "This isn't right."

"Really?" Reed didn't bother to take the sarcasm out of his voice, either. "Someone's tried to kill Addison and me twice. Someone succeeded in killing a woman, and her sister is now missing. Now Rooney's been shot—"

"No," the man interrupted. He stepped forward and held up something in his hand. Some kind of I.D.

When Reed went closer, he saw that it was credentials as a private investigator, including a photo I.D. But there was indeed something wrong. Because it was the guy's picture all right, but the name beneath it was none other than Blake Rooney.

"Is this some kind of sick joke?" Addison asked, and Reed realized that she'd not only come up behind him, but leaned in close enough to see the I.D.

"No joke," their visitor answered. And that wasn't a joking expression. "I'm the real Blake Rooney, and the guy who's been posing as me is Mitchell Cantor."

Their visitor paused, and that nonjoking expression got a heck of a lot worse. "And I think maybe he's the one who's been trying to kill you."

Chapter Thirteen

Addison heard what their visitor said, but there was so much about it that didn't make sense. Not the part about the man posing as Rooney perhaps being the one who was trying to kill them. The P.I. was a suspect, after all, so no surprise there.

However, why had the P.I. she'd hired pretended to be someone else in the first place?

Reed must have had the same question, because he aimed his index finger at the visitor. "Start explaining," he said at the same time that Cooper grumbled something about getting verification that this Rooney was who he claimed to be. Cooper went to a computer on Colt's desk.

The man nodded and blew out a long breath. "The guy's real name is Mitchell Cantor. We served in the military together. We're not friends exactly, but we've stayed in touch. Anyway, he paid me a visit about a couple of weeks ago and asked me to help him out with an investigation."

"This Cantor guy is a P.I., too?" Addison asked.

But Rooney quickly shook his head. "He got in trouble with the law after he left the military and couldn't get his P.I. license."

Great. He had a criminal record. And yes, she'd done

a quick computer check on Rooney, but his photo hadn't been on his website. She'd had no idea that she was dealing with an imposter.

"Rooney's driver's license photo matches the guy in front of us," Cooper said, looking up from the computer screen. "I'll call Pete and give him a heads-up that we might have trouble."

And trouble might come in the form of another attack. At least Cantor was hurt and wouldn't be able to do a lot of damage on his own. Or appeared to be hurt anyway. If his injury was fake, he'd done a good job of it. The blood had certainly seemed real.

But why would he have faked an injury?

Addison didn't have an answer for that, either.

"Pete said Cantor is with the E.R. doctor right now," Cooper relayed after he finished his call. "He'll talk to Cantor as soon as the doc's done. I told Pete to be careful, that Cantor might be dangerous."

Maybe Cantor would just come clean about being an imposter. While she was hoping, Addison added that the man would have answers to help them with the case.

However, he might be the exact reason there was a case.

"Cantor said he was staying here in town at a hotel. Any idea which one?" Reed asked Addison.

She had to shake her head.

"I'll make some more calls," Cooper offered.

While the sheriff got started with that, Reed turned back toward Rooney. "What's Cantor investigating, and why would you think he's the one who's been trying to kill us?"

The P.I. gathered his breath again. "Cantor's looking for a woman, Cissy Blanco," Rooney said. "I'm not sure exactly what his relationship with her was, but it's possible they were romantically involved."

Addison latched right on to that. "Did he father a baby she had two years ago?"

Rooney shrugged. "I have no idea. Cantor just wanted me to use my P.I. resources to track her down, but I got a bad feeling about it right off. Like maybe he was looking for her because he wanted to get back at her for something. So I told him I was too busy to help. Guess that's when he decided to steal my I.D. and go after her on his own."

"Cissy's dead," Reed provided. "She was murdered."

"I read about it in the paper," Rooney readily admitted, "and that's when I knew I had to do something. I went to SAPD, and Dominic was there on another matter. He said he was Cissy's lawyer and that I should come here and tell you about Cantor."

Dominic gave a crisp nod. "I knew something was wrong about Cantor from the moment I met him. I mean, why accuse me of being behind these attacks?" He didn't wait for an answer. "It was to throw suspicion off himself, that's why. He probably killed Cissy and then tried to kill you."

Maybe. It was a long shot, but maybe Cantor truly had been just looking for Cissy because he had feelings for her and had come across something incriminating about Dominic. Addison wasn't about to trust any of them at this point, but her distrust of Cantor was sky-high since he'd lied about his identity.

"Cantor probably knows we're onto him," the real Rooney continued. "I called him on the drive over here so I could confront him about what he was doing. He didn't answer, but I left him a voice mail. He's probably listened to that message by now."

"But I have his phone," Colt said, holding it up. "No calls or texts have come through in the past hour."

The moment Colt said that, Reed cursed. "Cantor could have had two phones. He probably gave us that one because he figured it would clear his name when we got in touch with his contacts."

And it did.

Or at least it would have done if the real Rooney hadn't shown up.

"I've got dispatch contacting the hotels in the area," Cooper said when he finished his call. "If we can find out where Cantor was staying, I'll have his room searched."

It was a good start. Cantor might have left something behind that could shed light on this. If he had any light to shed, that is. Addison silently groaned. They didn't need any more questions. Only answers.

"Judge Quarles knows about this, too," Rooney added a moment later. That got their attention, as well.

"Yes," Dominic verified. He turned to Addison. "Rooney told me about it on the drive over. Quarles knew you'd hired a fake P.I., and I'm guessing he didn't say a word to you about it."

"He didn't." And Addison intended to find out why he didn't. There was no logical reason for him to keep information like that to himself. If it was true, that is.

Addison had to keep reminding herself there were a lot of *ifs* in all this. Because the two people in front of her might not even be telling the truth.

"How did Quarles find out Cantor was a fake?" she asked Rooney.

Cooper's phone rang, and he stepped away to answer it, but he motioned for Rooney to continue talking.

"Late yesterday, Judge Quarles called out of the

blue," Rooney explained. "He said I sounded funny, nothing like the man he'd spoken with here in Sweetwater Springs. I told him I hadn't been in this town in years."

So Quarles had likely known for hours. Withholding the information didn't paint him in a good light. Of course, the judge would probably have a good explanation for what he'd done. Maybe that he hadn't had time to tell them, but Addison's theory went in a more sinister direction.

What if Quarles was behind Cissy's murder and had hoped Cantor would kidnap or kill her because of something Cissy had told her? A man who hid his real identity didn't usually do that unless he was up to no good, and Quarles might have hoped to capitalize on that.

"I called Quarles," Dominic went on. "I figured you'd want to talk to him, so he's on his way over."

Addison groaned, and this time it wasn't silent. Of course, she wanted to talk to Quarles, but after the day from Hades, she wasn't sure she was up to another round with the judge right now. Plus, there were arrangements for the safe houses that needed to be finalized, and that couldn't happen with any of their suspects around. Every minute they spent here was precious time her baby wasn't in a more protected place.

Cooper finished his latest call, his attention going straight to Reed. *Mercy.* Something else was wrong. Addison could tell from Cooper's expression.

"Reed and Addison, can I talk to you a minute, *alone?*" Cooper asked.

Definitely bad news, and Addison tried to brace herself when they stepped into Cooper's office.

"Someone stole the DNA for Mellie's baby," Cooper said, keeping his voice low.

Addison had expected something much worse, like another attack. Still, it wasn't good that someone had stolen the baby's DNA.

Except it did mean that the DNA was likely important.

"Can they just get another sample?" she asked. It would delay them getting the information, but at least they would know eventually.

"Maybe, if we can find the adoptive mother. She seems to have disappeared."

All right, so that was the *much worse* part. Addison prayed nothing bad had happened to the woman, but it was a strong possibility she'd been hurt or even killed. Someone definitely didn't want the baby's DNA to come to light, probably because it would implicate that *someone* in a whole boatload of serious crimes.

"I'll get Rooney's statement," Cooper offered. "Quarles, too, when he gets here. You two look exhausted. As soon as the safe houses are ready, I suggest you get out of here."

She could tell Reed wanted to argue with that. He no doubt wanted to stay and help with these new wrinkles in the investigation, but getting Emily to a safe house was their top priority right now. Besides, there were no guarantees they'd get anything helpful from Rooney, Dominic or Quarles. Their best bet right now seemed to be Cantor, and Pete had already agreed to question him.

Cooper went back into the squad room, and when Addison turned to follow him, Reed took hold of her arm. However, he didn't say anything until Cooper was out of earshot.

"I need to apologize," he whispered.

Addison didn't need him to clarify that. He was sorry about that kiss. Well, so was she.

Okay, partly.

She was sorry it was causing Reed to twist and turn inside. And that was exactly what he was doing. He would see the kiss as a massive lapse in judgment, but Addison knew that judgment had nothing to do with it.

"The divorce ended our marriage," she said, "not the heat that's always been between us."

With his gaze connected with hers, he made a sound of agreement, and for a moment Addison thought he was going to kiss her again. Or maybe it was just wishful thinking on her part. Oh, yes, she wanted more kisses from Reed, but she knew they would come at a high price. Not just for Reed.

But for her, too.

Reed was still wrestling with being a father. Still wrestling with having feelings for her that he didn't want to have. And he was doing all that while trying to keep Emily and her out of the path of a killer. However, when the danger was over, it was possible that Reed would embrace fatherhood but not her. He might never be able to forgive her for what she'd done.

That meant Addison could get her heart crushed again.

Yes, that kiss came at a very high price.

She heard the front door open. Heard the voices, too, and knew that Quarles had already arrived.

Oh, joy.

"I think you have your killer," Quarles was saying to Cooper when Reed and she went back into the squad room. "I hope you're about to arrest that imposter."

"My deputy will question him," Cooper explained. "And if there's a reason to arrest him, then we will."

While Cooper was still talking, the judge's attention

went to Addison. "You should do a better job of screening people you let into your life."

She flinched, but before she could say anything, Reed stepped in front of her. "You have a reason to be here, Judge Quarles?"

And he sounded about as friendly as Addison felt. She'd been a fool to trust Cantor, but she didn't need Quarles reminding her of that.

"Yes, I have a darn good reason," Quarles insisted. "Someone's trying to drag me into this baby farm mess, and I believe Addison started it all by hiring a fake P.I. I think Cantor's behind everything—the murder and the attacks—and he wants to frame me for it."

"And someone's doing the same to me," Dominic added.

"Please," Quarles said, stretching the word out. "You're a lawyer. If your reputation is sullied by these accusations, it'll barely make a ripple in your career. I, on the other hand, will be ruined. That's why the sheriff needs to make an arrest now so I can start putting all this behind me."

If only they had enough evidence for an arrest. But they didn't seem any closer now than when all this had begun.

"It won't help to arrest Cantor if he's only guilty of impersonating a P.I.," Reed argued. "There's a lot going on. Stuff that requires plenty of money and a strong motive. I'm not sure Cantor has either. Heck, I'm not even sure he's connected to Dearborn, the baby farms or the kidnapping attempts. He could have just been looking for a friend who's now been murdered."

Clearly, neither Dominic nor Quarles cared much for Reed's theory. Dominic belted out some profanity, and the anger flashed through the judge's eyes. But there was anger in Reed's eyes, too.

"You knew that Cantor was a fake, and you waited to tell us," Reed said to Quarles. "Why?"

That didn't help with the judge's angry response. "Great. Now you're back to accusing me of wrongdoing. You're not the only one with a full plate right now, Deputy. I didn't have time to tell you, but I'm telling you now—arrest Cantor, because he's a killer."

Reed and Cooper exchanged glances, and Addison could almost see what was going on in their heads. Cantor had been shot, maybe trying to catch the kidnappers. Maybe not.

Only Cantor would be able to tell them that.

"I'll have my deputy check on Cantor again," Cooper agreed. "But if the doctors say Cantor's not up to being questioned yet, then our little visit ends now so that Reed and I can get back to doing our jobs."

However, when Cooper reached for his phone, it rang before he could make the call to Pete. With all the bad news they'd gotten lately, Addison braced herself for another round, but she prayed that the danger had stayed away from Emily, the other babies and the Sweetwater Ranch.

Cooper didn't put the call on speaker. Nor did he say anything for several snail-crawling moments. "How bad?" he asked.

Addison's heart dropped. "Please, not Emily." And it took everything inside her to stay still and not run out to the ranch.

"You can't," Reed said, no doubt knowing what she was thinking. "It could be a trick to draw us out into the open again."

He was right, of course, but it still took a huge effort and Reed's grip to make her stay put.

"Secure the room and don't let anyone leave the hotel. I'll be right there," Cooper told the person on the other end of the line.

Even though this was obviously still bad news, Addison blew out the breath she'd been holding. This wasn't about Emily.

"You found Cantor's hotel room?" Reed asked the moment Cooper finished the call.

"Yeah, he was staying at the Bluebonnet Inn," Cooper verified. "And Mellie was there." A muscle flickered in his jaw. "An ambulance is on the way to her now."

Chapter Fourteen

Reed mentally repeated what Cooper had just told them, but there was one word that came through loud and clear.

Ambulance.

"Mellie's hurt?" Addison asked. Without even looking at Reed, she leaned against him. Probably because her legs felt like rubber. Yeah, Reed was feeling that, too, along with being sick to his stomach.

Cooper nodded and generally looked as disgusted with himself as Reed felt. "She's not conscious. The hotel clerk said it appears that she's been shot."

Good thing Addison was using him for support, because that did it. She didn't just lean against Reed. She sagged against him, and he hooked his arm around her waist to keep her from falling.

"Oh, God," Addison whispered. "This can't happen again."

But it apparently had happened again. This was yet another dose of bad news they didn't need. Especially Mellie. The young woman had been afraid for her life, and they'd failed her. They'd let someone, a shooter, get to her.

But who?

The most obvious answer was Cantor. Sometimes,

though, the most obvious wasn't the truth, because their other suspects, Dominic and Quarles, could have been the ones behind this, as well.

"But Mellie's alive?" Dominic asked.

Cooper nodded. "For now. The clerk said she's lost a lot of blood. She appears to have a head injury, too."

Hell. This just kept getting worse and worse.

"But she's alive," Dominic said. "That means she might be able to tell us who attacked her."

Dominic's breathing kicked up significantly, and he looked ready to bolt from the building. Maybe only because it was a reminder that the danger was so close. Just up the street.

Or maybe he looked that way because Mellie could implicate him in this.

"I told you Cantor was dangerous," Quarles spat out. Unlike Dominic, he didn't appear to be on the verge of panicking or running. He had an *I told you* so expression on his smug face. "He should be arrested *now*."

"Or someone setting him up could want to make him look dangerous," Reed argued. "Cantor hasn't exactly spent a lot of time in his hotel room, so it's not likely he was the one who shot Mellie." Though it was possible that was exactly what he'd done.

Still, it would mean the man had either left the chase for the kidnapper or shot Mellie before he even drove out to the spot of the attack. But if Cantor had been the one to shoot her in order to silence her, then why had he done it in his own hotel room? And as chilling as it was to consider, why hadn't Cantor made sure he'd succeeded? Even an amateur killer would have ensured that his intended victim was dead so she couldn't identify him.

"Why was Mellie there in Cantor's hotel room anyway?" Dominic asked no one in particular. "She was worried about her safety, so why did she go to him instead of the police?"

Reed didn't know for sure, but it was possible Mellie didn't trust the cops. After all, they hadn't done such a good job of protecting her sister. But why had she thought she could trust Cantor? What kind of history did those two have that would make her go to his hotel room?

Or maybe he'd somehow lured her there?

"You said Cantor was looking for Cissy," Reed reminded Rooney. "What specifically did he want you to do to help him?"

"He wanted files from Dearborn," Rooney answered without hesitating. "He also wanted me to try to get surveillance feed from the traffic camera just outside Cissy's apartment."

Quarles froze. For just a split second. "Did you get it for him?"

"I couldn't. The traffic camera wasn't working for the time period he wanted."

Too bad because that surveillance footage might have shown them who'd visited Cissy. That, in turn, could have given possible answers about her killer.

"Did Cantor say anything else about why he wanted to find Cissy?" Addison pressed.

Rooney shook his head. "I'm sorry, and I didn't push him for more, either. Like I said, I thought maybe she was an old girlfriend or something."

"I'll go to the hospital to talk to Cantor," Colt volunteered. But then he stopped and looked at Rooney. "Unless you think this is some kind of attempt to get us apart so the kidnappers can come after Addison again."

That didn't help the sick feeling in Reed's stomach.

Because it could be true. What he needed was to press to get those safe houses ready. However, he had no intention of doing that until he got rid of this trio.

"Have Pete talk to Cantor now," Cooper instructed Colt. "And have him make sure Cantor is kept away from Mellie when the ambulance brings her in." Cooper turned to Reed. "You can use my office to check on those plans being made. In the meantime, I'll make sure our visitors find their way out."

Reed didn't wait for a second invitation. Since he wanted her away from Dominic and Quarles, he got Addison moving in the direction of Cooper's office. Once they were in the hall, he checked over his shoulder to make sure the others had left. Dominic had. But Quarles and Rooney were at the door, talking. That probably wasn't a good sign, but for now Reed had Addison sit down, and he took out his phone to call the marshal's service about the safe houses.

Finally, he got some good news.

"The houses are ready," Reed relayed to Addison as soon as he got off the phone. "And as requested the marshals beefed up the protection detail for Emily." Reed would do the beefing up himself for Addison's protection.

There was a glimmer of relief in her eyes. Quickly followed by fear and dread. Yes, Emily would be safe. Or at least *safer.* But it meant Addison was going to have to say goodbye to their little girl.

"She won't be away from you for long," Reed assured her. Maybe that wasn't a lie. "Come on. Let's go to the ranch and wait until the marshals arrive to pick her up."

It wouldn't take the marshals much time to make it there. Probably about an hour, and each minute of the hour would seem like an eternity to him, because during that time both Addison and Emily would still be in danger.

Reed led her back into the hall and was glad to see that both Rooney and Quarles had finally left. However, Cooper was on the phone, and he held up his finger in a *wait a second* gesture.

"I'll get there as fast as I can," Cooper said to the caller.

That stopped Reed in his tracks. "What's wrong now?" he asked the moment Cooper finished the call.

"A gunman wearing a mask got into the hospital and forced Cantor to leave with him."

"Is Pete okay?" Addison wanted to know.

"He's fine. Just riled." Cooper grabbed his Stetson and headed for the door. "Pete's in pursuit, but you should probably wait here until I'm back so I can escort you to the ranch."

Cooper hurried out before Reed could remind him that waiting around anywhere wasn't a good idea. Of course, neither was going out there without backup.

"I wouldn't get near the windows," Colt reminded him, and he went to the front door and locked it.

Addison and Reed moved back into the hall, and the waiting began. Again. How the devil had this happened? The small country hospital didn't have security. Didn't usually need it. But Pete had been there to prevent anything bad from happening.

"How could the gunman have gotten past Pete?" he asked, knowing she wouldn't have the answer. "He would have been watching the E.R. entrance to make sure no one came in that way."

"Maybe the person got in through one of the clinics." Addison rubbed her hand down his arm.

Her arm rub was no doubt an attempt to try to reassure him, but no gesture could do that. However, the clinic entrance theory did make sense, since they were offices attached to the hospital but with their own private entrances. At this time of day, anyone could have gone through one of those clinics and waltzed into the hospital. And into the room where Cantor was being examined.

"There's only one reason a masked gunman would go after Cantor," Reed said. "And that's to silence him. Maybe because Cantor got a look at the kidnapper after all."

Addison made a sound of agreement. "And maybe this gunman was the one who attacked Mellie." That brought her fingers to her mouth. "Oh, God. Mellie could be dying."

And probably was. In fact, the person who shot her had likely left her for dead or else had been interrupted while trying to kill her.

No way could Reed confirm that, though. "Maybe this gunman who took Cantor is a ruse that Cantor himself set up so he'd look innocent."

"You think he staged his own injury, too?" she asked.

Reed nodded. "It's possible. The person behind this is facing capital murder charges. Cantor might go to any lengths to keep from getting the death penalty. Plus, if he hired this gunman to come into the hospital, it means Cantor's not around to have to answer any other questions. Especially now that we all know he lied about being Rooney."

Addison stayed quiet a moment and then gasped. "Cantor and the gunman could be coming here to attack us again." But then she shook her head as if reconsidering that. "If Cantor wanted to kill me, he had his chance when he staggered into the sheriff's office."

Yeah, he had. Cantor could have just come in with guns blazing. Maybe that meant he didn't want to kill Addison.

Not yet anyway.

But why had Cantor come to the sheriff's office in the first place? It didn't make sense.

Outside in the squad room, Reed heard Colt's phone ring, and he stepped into the doorway, hoping to hear an update on Cantor or Mellie. The woman had to be at the hospital by now. Alive, hopefully.

But Reed immediately rethought that when Colt cursed. "We're on our way," he said.

Colt pivoted in Reed's direction. "Someone just fired shots at the ranch."

ADDISON COULDN'T CATCH her breath. Couldn't speak, either. But that didn't stop her from running out of Cooper's office. It didn't matter there might be kidnappers outside, waiting for her.

The only thing that mattered now was getting to Emily.

"Stop!" Colt shouted to them. "I'm coming with you. I'll have the dispatcher get Shawna and Jasper in here ASAP to man the office."

She hated to wait even the few seconds that it took Colt to do that, but they might need all the firepower they could get.

"Who called and how bad it is?" Reed asked as they hurried out the back of the building. He also drew his gun.

"Darnell was the one who called." Colt didn't stop moving. He locked the back door and got them running toward his truck that was parked nearest to the building. He, too, pulled his weapon. "Three shots were fired.

None came into the house, but at least one hit the fence at the front of the property."

Thank God the bullets hadn't gone into the house where Emily and the others were, but it'd been a minute or more since Darnell, one of the ranch hands, called Colt with the news about the shooting.

There was no telling what had gone on in that minute.

With all the bad things that'd happened in the past twenty-four hours, Addison's mind went in the direction of a worst-case scenario. But she couldn't bear the thoughts that came. She had to focus on getting to the ranch.

"Stay low on the seat," Reed warned her.

She did, but he didn't. Colt got behind the wheel and drove away from the sheriff's office while Reed kept watch all around them. There was a good reason for that. This could all be a ruse to draw them out into the open.

If so, it'd worked.

There was no way Addison would stay tucked away with Emily and the rest of the McKinnons in danger.

"I'll check with Darnell to see what's going on," Colt said, making the call while they sped out of town.

The ranch was only about twenty minutes away. Not that far. But each mile would feel like an eternity.

"I'm calling Rosalie," Addison insisted, and she pulled Reed's phone from his pocket.

Thankfully, Rosalie answered on the first ring.

"Emily's safe," Rosalie said before Addison could even ask. "Austin and I are in the bathroom at the main house with Emily and our baby. We'll make sure no one gets in here."

Austin was an FBI agent and well trained to deal

with situations like this. And Addison figured the bathroom was the safest place. The bullets would have a harder time going through the tile and natural stone in the McKinnon bathrooms.

Still, nothing felt safe right now.

"Have there been any more shots fired?" Addison held her breath, prayed.

"No. And the ranch hands are guarding the house and out looking for the shooter. Rayanne's husband, Blue, is keeping watch, too."

Blue McCurdy was yet another lawman. Addison was thankful for him and all the others, but she still wouldn't be able to fight off the panic until she was holding her baby in her arms.

Addison heard a sound that caused that panic to spike.

Emily crying.

"She's okay," Rosalie volunteered quickly, "but I need to give her a bottle. Honestly, this is the first sound she's made since we brought her in here. And try not to worry. I'll call you if anything changes."

Addison hated for the call to end, but she also wanted Emily to get the attention she needed to soothe her nerves. Yes, she was just a baby, but she had to sense the tension around her. Addison certainly felt it. Every muscle in Reed's body was primed for a fight.

"There haven't been any other shots fired," Addison relayed to Reed once she ended the call with Rosalie.

Colt ended his call, too, but he shook his head. "Darnell and the others haven't been able to find the shooters."

"Shooters?" Reed growled. "Exactly how many are there?"

"Darnell thinks there are two of them. All three shots

came from the wooded area at the front of the ranch. Probably fired from long-range rifles. One shot came from the east side. The other two came from the west."

One gunman was bad enough, but now there were two.

Or maybe even more.

"We can't just go driving into the ranch," Colt added a moment later. "More gunmen could be waiting there to ambush us."

That caused the skin to crawl on her neck—it could be exactly what these gunmen had planned, because they were in the perfect position to come after them. Judging from where those shots had originated, the gunmen were across from the road that Colt would have to use to get them to the ranch house.

Colt would literally have to drive right by the shooters.

"We'll have to approach this slowly," Reed reminded her. "We might even have to wait for the gunmen to be found, because we can't do anything that would make them start firing again."

Her breath caught in her throat. Yes, she did know that. But Addison also knew she had to get to Emily.

"The ranch hands have fanned out," Colt said. "They're all looking for the shooters. We will, too, but we'll do it from the end of the road. That way, if they fire, the shots will come at us and not toward the house."

Reed cursed. Because he knew it was true—that they were right back in the middle of danger again.

That couldn't be helped.

If she could save her baby by drawing fire away from the house, then that was exactly what Addison would do.

The minutes and miles crawled by, and by the time they reached the final turn toward Sweetwater Ranch,

Addison's muscles were so tight that her entire body was aching. Her head was pounding, too. And she thought she might pass out from holding her breath so long. Still, she forced herself to focus. To listen for any sounds or movement that those shooters might make.

Instead of taking the ranch road, Colt eased the truck to a stop on the shoulder, and Reed and he both looked around them. Addison tried to do the same, but Reed pushed her back down on the seat.

"I don't see anything," Reed said to Colt. "You?"

Colt shook his head and reached for his phone. "I'll get an update from Darnell."

But Colt had no sooner said that than she felt Reed stiffen even more than he already was. "There," he said, tipping his head to the wooded area across from the ranch.

Exactly where Darnell had said the shooters had fired from.

"I see him," Colt answered.

Even though she was already low on the seat, Reed pushed her to the floor, and in the same motion, he turned his gun in the direction where both Colt and he were now looking. Neither of them fired, but both had their fingers positioned over their triggers.

Colt's phone rang, and without taking his attention off the wooded area, he motioned for Addison to answer it. She did, but she didn't put it on speaker because she didn't want the sound of the caller's voice to prevent Colt and Reed from possibly hearing an approaching gunman.

"It's me, Addison," she answered in a whisper when she saw Darnell's name on the screen.

"Tell Colt we have eyes on the shooter on the west side of the property," Darnell said.

"We're at the end of the road, and Colt and Reed have eyes on the other one."

If there were only two of them, that meant they were both covered. However, there could be heaven knows how many attackers out there.

"Please tell me someone's guarding the back of the ranch so these goons can't get on the grounds," she said to Darnell.

"Roy and Tucker are back there."

Colt's dad and his brother, a Texas Ranger. Good. That was firepower in the exact place it might be needed. There were old ranch trails that ran at the back of McKinnon land.

"Tell Colt that me and a couple of the guys are moving in on the shooter that we're watching," Darnell added. "Once we're done with him, we'll head your way."

Since her hands were shaking so hard, it took Addison several attempts to hit the end call button, and she relayed Darnell's message. Reed groaned, clearly not happy about playing sitting duck or helping Darnell, but at the moment it was the only option they had.

So they waited.

Addison tried to block out the memory of Emily crying. A sound she'd heard just minutes earlier when she'd talked to Rosalie. Hard to make the cries go away, however, especially when nothing was certain right now.

Nothing was safe.

But that would change. The safe houses were ready, and if they got out of this unscathed, Addison would make sure Emily was taken to one of the houses immediately. Far away from her and any place where the attackers would find her. That broke Addison's heart, but it would break even more if she didn't do whatever it took to get her baby out of harm's way.

Even though she'd tried to brace herself for whatever might happen next, Addison still jumped and gasped when she heard the sound of the gunfire. Not directly nearby but in the area of the woods where Darnell had said he'd spotted the gunman. It wasn't a single shot but several.

Oh, God. A gunfight.

She prayed those bullets would stay away from the house.

Colt and Reed continued to fire glances all around them. Waiting. With his partner under fire, the gunman on their end of the woods might start shooting, too. And if he did, maybe Colt and Reed could put an end to this.

Well, an end to the immediate danger anyway.

If they killed both gunmen, they wouldn't get answers as to who'd sent them, but at the moment, Addison didn't care about that. She just wanted this to end so she could get Emily to safety.

"You hear that?" Reed asked.

Addison hadn't heard anything other than the gunfire, but she lifted her head just a little.

It was the sound of an engine, and it wasn't the truck because Colt had turned it off. This sound was coming from the road just to the side of the woods.

"Hell," Reed mumbled. "The gunman's getting away."

Part of Addison was glad the idiot was escaping, but if he did get away, it would mean that he'd just come back for another attack.

Reed threw open the truck door and stepped out, taking aim at the vehicle. She couldn't see it, but judging from the sound, it was rapidly approaching.

Reed fired, but judging from the profanity he started mumbling, his shot had missed. Addison heard the other vehicle speed away.

"Did you get a look at him?" Colt asked.

"Yeah," Reed answered, jumping back in the truck. "There were two men. And Cantor was one of them."

Chapter Fifteen

So much was coming at Reed right now. Finding Cantor and that gunman. Getting answers about this latest attack. But all those things were pushed to the back burner when he saw the marshals putting Emily into the car. The car that would take his baby to the safe house.

Away from Addison and him.

Colt was on the phone, searching for some of those answers they desperately needed. Cooper was back at the sheriff's office doing the same thing. However, the ranch would stay on lockdown until both Addison and Emily were in their respective safe houses.

Addison had already kissed the baby goodbye more than a dozen times, but she kissed her again. Tears continued to spill down Addison's cheeks. Reed could practically feel her heart breaking, but they both knew they didn't have another choice. One of the kidnappers was dead, but the other was at large, and Reed figured he wasn't working alone.

No way.

Cantor or whoever else was behind this would be back to finish the job. Well, their attacker would try anyway. But Reed had every intention of stopping him and anyone else involved.

Addison and Emily had been through enough.

"You want to say goodbye to Emily?" Addison asked Reed.

Not really. Reed wanted to be with her instead, but that was impossible. For now anyway.

He went closer, hating that sick feeling of dread in the pit of his stomach. How could someone so little cause such a firestorm of emotions inside him? How could he love anyone this much after only knowing her two days?

And he did love her.

There was no mistaking that.

Reed leaned in and brushed a kiss on Emily's forehead. She was asleep but stirred a little and opened one eye to peek out at him. Even though she was way too young to understand what was going on, Reed tried to put on a strong face for her.

"I'll have you home soon, sweet girl," he whispered to her.

It was a bold promise, especially since he wasn't even sure where home was for her. They hadn't exactly had any downtime to talk about living arrangements and such, but Reed knew that somehow he'd be a big part of Emily's life.

Addison kissed the baby one last time, and the four marshals and the bodyguard nanny got into the SUV with her. It was a strong protection detail with twice the number of people usually involved. Reed had insisted on that because he didn't want to take any more chances with Emily's safety.

Marshal Dallas Walker got behind the wheel of the SUV and looked out at Reed. "As soon as I have them settled and I'm sure all is well, I'll be back to escort Addison to her safe house."

Reed nodded and managed to mumble thanks despite the thick lump that formed in his throat. That lump only got worse as he watched Marshal Walker drive away. He put his arm around Addison, figuring she'd need it.

She did.

Because she practically collapsed against him.

"It might take hours for the marshal to get to the safe house and then get back here," Colt reminded them. "Why don't y'all come inside until then?"

It was a generous offer, but Reed figured Addison wouldn't be comfortable there. Yes, Roy didn't seem upset about her friendship with Jewell, but Addison didn't need anything else adding to her stress.

Reed glanced over at the guesthouse. "What about there? Can we use that place instead?"

Addison shook her head before Colt could answer. "Rosalie's brother is staying there."

"He's in San Antonio working a case and won't be back for a day or two. Use the guesthouse," Colt insisted. "You both need a break even if it's only for a few hours. Get some rest."

Getting rest and being tucked away were the last things Reed wanted right now. He wanted to be in the thick of the investigation, but it was obvious that Addison needed to get off her feet. She was a lightweight drinker, so maybe he could even talk her into a shot of whiskey, just enough to relax her so she could take a nap.

Of course, that was asking a lot from mere whiskey.

Until she had Emily back safe and sound, he figured neither one of them would be doing much resting. Still, he took Colt up on the offer, thanked him and led Addison toward the guesthouse.

"You saw Cantor in the getaway car," she said.

Reed hadn't been sure how much she'd heard of what he'd told Colt and Cooper. She had been seemingly focused just on Emily after they arrived at the ranch. Obviously, she'd heard that part, though.

"I saw him in the passenger seat," Reed verified. "But I couldn't tell if he was a captive or a willing participant." Cantor would no doubt say he was the latter. And maybe he was. "He didn't look too well. Definitely like a man who'd been shot and had left the hospital too soon."

That still didn't make him innocent in all this.

If Addison hadn't been in the truck with Colt and him, Reed would have gone in pursuit and perhaps finally gotten the answers that could stop another attack. The dead kidnapper certainly couldn't tell them much, but once they had an I.D. on him, maybe they could connect him to one of their suspects.

Quarles, Dominic or Cantor.

Reed opened the door to the guesthouse and didn't waste any time getting Addison to the sofa. Didn't waste time on the drink, either, though he also poured one for himself. He wasn't exactly an old pro when it came to handling gunfire, but he'd had to deal with some situations. However, it'd never rattled him like this before.

Of course, the stakes had never been this high, either.

"You and Colt got an update on Mellie while I was saying goodbye to Emily," Addison muttered. She took a sip of the whiskey and grimaced. Yeah, definitely not much of a drinker.

"Mellie's still alive." And that was somewhat of a miracle. After all, she'd been shot in the head. "She's in surgery."

The alarm flashed through Addison's eyes. "Her attacker could come after her—"

"Pete's guarding her, and we've requested assistance from law enforcement in nearby towns. We'll make sure she's not left alone."

There would be so much protection if the idiots came after Mellie, then they'd get caught. Reed was all for that as long as no more harm was done to innocent people—and for him, Mellie fell into that category.

"It's all too much." As if she didn't know what to do with herself, Addison stood and paced to the front window. Then the back. "The marshal really will call as soon as he's at the safe house, right?"

Reed nodded, confirming something that Addison already knew. Emily was in good hands, but neither Reed nor she would rest easy until they got that call.

He watched her do the nervous pacing, and when she was on her fourth round, Reed stepped in front of her. His intention was for her to stop. And she did. By plowing right into him.

Suddenly, his arms were filled with Addison, and his arms clearly thought that was a darn good thing.

It wasn't.

Ditto for what happened next. Addison didn't step away from him, something she'd gotten really good at doing. Nope. She didn't use that particular skill set here. She stayed put, her body right against him.

Yeah, he got some bad idea as to what to do about that.

She looked up at him. Blinked. Because she was so close, she picked up the rhythm of his breathing, and like the body contact, she didn't do a thing to break the eye contact, either. Of course, Reed was pretty much doing nothing, either. Well, nothing except drinking her in as if she were his for the drinking.

Their breaths didn't help things. As his chest rose, so

did her breasts. More touching. And yes, she noticed, but he was pretty sure he noticed first.

There was a storm brewing inside him now, but it was a storm of a different kind. All fire and heat.

All bad.

Because he could go *there* with Addison, but that didn't mean he should.

"I'm having the same battle," she whispered. No need to clarify. They both knew exactly what was happening.

"Are you winning?" he asked.

She shook her head. "You?"

He lifted his eyebrow. "I'm a guy. We never win battles like this."

But this was more than just a *guy* kind of thing. This was Addison, looking like silk and sin. Probably feeling like it, too. He knew every inch of her.

And he wanted to know it all over again.

"I think we just lost the battle," she said, her whispered breath hitting against his mouth.

Yeah. They'd lost it minutes ago, and Reed was bright enough to admit it and do what he couldn't stop himself from doing.

Taking Addison.

So that was what he did. Reed lowered his head and kissed her, and it was all they needed to get them both moving in the wrong direction. Because it didn't take much of a kiss for them to know that a kiss wasn't going to satisfy much of anything. He'd been over a year without her, and his body was yelling that reminder to him.

Addison jumped right into the action with some kisses to his neck. Reed let that kick up the old heat inside him while he backed his way to the door and locked it. Best not to have any of the McKinnons walking in on this because Addison was determined to get his shirt off.

Reed would have helped if he hadn't been so determined to get hers off.

They managed to keep up the breakneck speed of the body kisses while they grappled with the tops. Reed won. And he tossed hers aside so he could go after her bra. The moment he had her breasts free, that was the direction where he took the kisses.

His shirt was only partly off, with just one arm free, but Addison stopped her clothing removal efforts when he took her nipple into his mouth.

She made a wicked little sound. Part pleasure, part relief.

The pleasure smacked into Reed, too, and it upped the pace. A lot. Addison pulled at his clothes as if they were in some kind of speed contest. Reed played that game as well, but he slowed when he finally got her naked.

She was perfect.

Like always.

But then their trouble had never been about a lack of attraction. The proof of that was in her hot gaze and searching hands. Her hands found pay dirt when she unzipped him and slid her fingers around his erection.

Now it was Reed's turn to make that sound of pleasure, though his lacked the silk of Addison's.

Her fingers worked some magic and made this seem even more urgent than it already was. So urgent that Reed felt himself sliding down to the floor with her. His back landed against the door. Addison landed against him on his lap.

Exactly where he wanted her. Especially since she was naked.

She freed him from his boxers and in the same motion took him inside her. Finally, things slowed. For just a few moments. That was because the pleasure nearly blinded him, and Reed lost his breath. It didn't matter. Nothing did at this point except taking this even further.

And they did.

Reed caught on to her hips, moving her in the rhythmic motion that would make this end way too soon. Of course, if it lasted too long they'd both probably pass out from the lack of breath and the breakneck pace.

There was a huge advantage in their positions. It put them face-to-face. So he could see Addison when she got close to shattering. He could also kiss her. Something that Reed did just as he pushed into her one last time.

And she did shatter with that kiss.

With her mouth on his, their bodies slick with sweat and the world spinning like crazy, Addison slipped right over the edge.

Not alone.

Reed was right there with her.

ADDISON DIDN'T HAVE to give all this much thought to know that it'd been a bad idea.

Well, it'd been a bad idea for Reed anyway. For her, it'd been an incredible reminder of just how good they could be together.

A reminder she didn't need.

She'd always known that. Had always known she'd blown their marriage when she went behind his back to take those dangerous fertility drugs. And now she knew that having sex with him wasn't going to fix anything.

In fact, it would make things worse.

This would be yet something else to add to Reed's

already full plate. Something that would make him feel guilty for giving her false hope that things could somehow be mended between them. But after nearly being killed several times and having her baby in the middle of gunfire, Addison had no intention of having false hope.

Or even real hope.

Even if she was still in love with her ex-husband.

Great.

This was not the best time to realize that with the pleasure still vibrating through her body. Mercy, he smelled good. Looked even better. And both of those were things that were better pushed aside.

Addison eased away from him and got up so she could gather her clothes. However, Reed took hold of her hand and pulled her back to him.

"Uh-oh. I know that look," he said. "It's called regret."

Yes, but surprisingly she didn't see the same look on his face. "I'm not sure what I'm seeing in your expression," she countered. "Was this a reminder that making love to me became a chore?" she asked.

"A chore," Reed repeated. This time he gave her a different look. As if she'd sprouted an extra head or something. "Making love to you could be called plenty of things but never a chore."

"Not even when we were working so hard to make a baby?"

"Even then." He shrugged, tried to scowl. It was somewhat diminished by the fact that he was nearly naked.

She waited, wondering if they were finally about to have that heart-to-heart that he'd been avoiding since their divorce, but he only grumbled something she didn't catch and let go of her hand so he could start dressing.

Almost immediately, the peep show went away after he pulled on his jeans. Then he reached for his shirt to cover up that toned, perfect chest. Addison picked up her clothes, too, but because she'd shed more of her things in the foreplay frenzy, Reed finished ahead of her and took out his phone.

"I'll call Colt and see if there's an update on Mellie's condition," he said. "Or anything else."

It was too soon for Marshal Walker to have reached the safe house with Emily and the others. The marshal had told them that he would have to drive around for a while to make sure they weren't being followed. Still, Addison moved closer to Reed so she could hear if there was any news. However, she couldn't tell much, since Reed remained silent after he asked about Mellie.

"Thanks," Reed said to Colt several moments later, and he took a deep breath before he turned to her. "Mellie made it out of surgery. She's critical but stable."

Though it was a long shot, Addison had to ask, "Has she said anything about her attacker?"

"Not yet." He sounded more hopeful than his expression indicated.

Still, they had to stay positive. Unless they caught one of the kidnappers and got information from him, Mellie was their best chance at learning who had succeeded in nearly murdering her. Because her attacker was likely the same person who'd gone after Reed, Emily and her.

Before Reed even had time to put his phone away, it rang again. Just like that, her mind came up with all kinds of worst-case scenarios. It was too soon for Marshal Walker to call them.

Unless something had gone wrong.

This time, Addison moved even closer to Reed, and her heart sank when she saw Unknown Caller on the screen.

Was the kidnapper calling to say that he'd taken Emily?

"It's me," the man said the moment Reed hit the answer button.

Cantor.

"I know what you're thinking," Cantor continued, "that I'm guilty of trying to kill you. But I didn't."

"You were in that car by the Sweetwater Ranch," Reed fired back, putting the call on speaker. "I saw you."

"I wasn't there voluntarily. I was kidnapped at gunpoint from the hospital, thrown into that car and driven to the ranch. I didn't have anything to do with that attack or the others."

"Really?" Reed snapped. "Then who did fire those shots?"

Cantor groaned. "I don't know. That sounds like a lie, but it's the truth. The guy wore a mask, and he drugged me. I could barely see my hand in front of my face much less make out who had me."

Addison latched right on to that. *"Had?"*

"When the drugs wore off, I managed to bash him in the head with a flashlight that I found on the floor of the car. I hit him hard a couple of times, but he was still conscious and tried to shoot me again. I got out and started running."

Again, Reed made no sound to indicate he believed him. With reason. Canton had lied about his identity from the get-go.

"Where are you?" Reed asked.

Cantor didn't jump to answer. "I'd rather not tell you in case your place is bugged. Whoever's trying to kill me nearly succeeded, again, and I'd rather not go another round with a killer."

"Same here. Where are you?" Reed repeated.

"I'll meet you at the sheriff's office in Sweetwater Springs. I need to check on someone first."

"Mellie?" Reed provided. "Because she's not at your hotel room."

"Where is she?" Either Cantor was faking his surprise or else he truly hadn't heard that she'd been shot. Of course, it was in his best interest to pretend to be surprised. After all, he was also a suspect in the woman's attack.

"She's safe," Reed said. "Now tell me about Cissy. Did you father her baby?"

"No." Cantor cursed, repeated his answer. "Nothing like that. She was a sweet kid. More like a sister, you know. I knew she was in some kind of trouble, and I just wanted to help her." He groaned. "Now somebody killed her."

"You're sure that somebody wasn't you?" Reed snapped.

"I'm sure," Cantor snapped back. "I don't expect you to believe me, but I loved her. No way would I have ever hurt her. Not Mellie, either. We aren't close the way Cissy and I were, but Cissy would have wanted me to look after Mellie. And that's what I was trying to do. That's why I had her come to my hotel room. I didn't think anyone would look for her there."

Maybe. But Cantor had a big reason to lie about this. He could be charged with Cissy's murder. And maybe he tried to kill Mellie because she'd learned the truth about him—that he was her sister's killer.

"About that meeting at the sheriff's office," Reed continued, "go there and turn yourself in."

Addison figured Cantor would have some kind of excuse as to why he couldn't do that. But it wasn't an argument she heard.

"Hell. They found me," Cantor mumbled.

Before he could say more, Addison heard another sound from the other end of the line that she definitely didn't want to hear.

Gunshots.

Chapter Sixteen

"Cantor?" Reed shouted into the phone, but he was talking to himself, because the man had already hung up.

Or maybe Cantor had been forced to hang up because someone had shot him again.

Of course, all this could be some kind of ploy to draw Addison and him out into the open. Reed wasn't about to fall for it again. They'd nearly been killed the last time.

He pressed in Colt's number and was about to relay the details of his conversation with Cantor, but Colt spoke before Reed could say anything.

"We got a problem. A couple of them," Colt added quickly. "Marshal Walker called and said someone's been following him the whole drive to the safe house."

"Oh, God." Even though Reed didn't have the call on speaker, Addison obviously heard every word. "Is Emily okay?" she asked.

"She's fine." But Colt didn't seem very certain of that. "There's not just one vehicle but two following the SUV. The marshal's tried to shake them, but he doesn't want to have to get into a situation where he has to outrun these guys, so he's headed back here to the sheriff's office."

"Not good," Reed said as fast as he could. "Cantor's on the way there, too, and he could have kidnappers on his tail."

Colt cursed. "Then we have no choice but to return to the ranch."

Reed didn't like that idea at all, but the problem was there was no totally safe place for Emily. Or for Addison. Still, he couldn't have the marshal driving around, trying to shake attackers who might try to take the baby.

"Yes, bring her here," Addison insisted.

But Reed didn't jump to agree to that. He first had to think through the logistics of this. The kidnappers had used the wooded area in front of the ranch to attack them, and they could already be out there, ready to do it again.

"Emily's out there with the kidnappers," Addison reminded him. Not that he needed a reminder. This situation was bad right now, but it could get even uglier if the kidnappers started firing shots when the SUV arrived.

"What about the back road to the ranch, the one that runs up behind the land that Rosalie and her husband are clearing for their new house?" Reed asked. "It's gated off."

And it didn't have nearly as many trees behind which the gunmen could hide.

"Yeah," Colt answered. "I could get a couple of the armed ranch hands over there to open the gate and make sure it's safe."

Reed would want more than a couple of men with guns. He'd want as many ranch hands as they could spare, because once the marshal drove in, the kidnappers might try to follow.

But that left them with another huge problem.

"The kidnappers could still attack the front of the ranch," Reed said. "I don't want anyone getting hurt."

Or worse, a two-prong attack where they'd all be caught in the middle.

Colt stayed quiet a moment, obviously giving that some thought.

"I can draw the kidnappers out," Addison volunteered. "It's me they want. If they see me, they won't go after anyone else, including Emily or a member of Colt's family."

Reed gave her a flat look to let her know that he'd just nixed her suggestion.

However, it did give Reed an idea.

"We need to secure the front of the ranch," he said to Colt. "And we could allow the kidnappers to follow the marshal through the gate on the back road. Once the SUV carrying Emily has gotten safely out of the way, then we could close in on whoever's following them."

"That might work," Colt finally said. "There are two old hay barns, just off the ranch road, and we could use one of them for cover. If the kidnappers follow the SUV onto the grounds, we could close the gate, trapping them."

"Not with Emily anywhere nearby," Addison protested.

"She won't be," Reed answered. "We can have the marshal take her to Cooper's house." It was only about a hundred yards from the main house, but in case the kidnappers made it onto the ranch grounds, there were no outbuildings near Cooper's place that they could use to hide in or launch an ambush from.

"What about Cooper's wife and son?" Addison asked, shaking her head.

"They aren't there," Colt said. "They're in San Antonio visiting friends."

Good. Of course, Rosalie, her baby and Roy were in

the main house, but maybe they could get them into a secure location like one of the bathrooms.

"Marshal Walker just sent me a text," Colt interrupted. "He said we need to hurry, that he's only about ten minutes out from the ranch."

That did it. Reed would have liked more time to work out the kinks in this plan they'd just slapped together, but every moment that he delayed meant Emily was out there.

"Call the marshal," Reed said to Colt. "Tell him that we need at least twenty minutes to get everyone in place. I'll call the ranch hands."

And anyone else he could trust to make sure things didn't go to hell in a handbasket.

"I can help," Addison said the moment he got off the phone. "Give me a gun, because I want to be in the barn to stop the kidnappers."

Reed brushed a kiss on her forehead and thanked her for her offer. "You're going to Cooper's house to wait for Emily to arrive. That's the best way you can help," he added when she started to argue.

She probably would have still tried to continue that argument, but Reed started those calls. "Use the landline to call Roy and let him know what's going on," he told her. "I want Rosalie, him, the baby and anyone else in the house far away from the windows."

While Addison did that, Reed got started with his own calls. First, to the ranch hand Darnell so he could assemble a group to go out to the gate and barns at the back of the ranch. Other ranch hands would go to the front of the property in case this was all a diversion by the kidnappers so they could try to take Addison.

"Rosalie's husband and Roy are both armed," Addison relayed to him once she finished her call to the main house. "They'll stay put until they hear from you."

Good. While he would have liked having Rosalie's FBI husband as backup, it was best if he stayed in the house to protect Rosalie and the others inside. Now Reed had to make sure the kidnappers didn't get that far onto the ranch.

"Cooper and Colt are on their way," Reed told her. "Colt will come with me. Cooper will be at his house with Emily, you and the marshal." Plus, there was the nanny-bodyguard and the others in the protection detail. Reed wished he had an entire army to put there, but at least Emily and Addison would be surrounded by people trained to keep them safe.

And that meant it was time to put these final pieces into place.

Pieces that would involve some more risks.

"I need to get you to Cooper's house so I can go to the barn," he said to her. "Some of the ranch hands are headed down to the front to keep an eye on that wooded area, but it's still possible that gunmen are hiding in there."

She gave a nod. Not a shaky one, either. "I want to be at Cooper's house when Emily gets there."

Where both of them would be away from possible trouble.

He hoped.

First, though, he had to get Addison there, and that meant taking her out in the open. That was where the risk part came in. Because a guy with a high-powered rifle could manage to shoot them the moment they stepped outside.

"Move fast," he instructed. "When you get in the truck, stay down, and I'll drive you to Cooper's house."

It wasn't far, less than a five-minute walk, but it would be harder for a gunman to hurt her if she was in the truck.

However, they'd hardly made it a step when Reed's phone rang again, and he answered it right away when he saw Colt's name on the screen.

"We've got a big problem," Colt said immediately. "Someone's firing at the SUV carrying Emily. Marshal Walker's heading to the ranch. You need to get to the back ranch gate *now.*"

ADDISON'S HEARTBEAT WENT into overdrive. So did the horrible images of what was possibly happening. The nightmarish thoughts came again, hard and fast like the bullets those monsters were firing at her baby.

"I'm going with you," she insisted before Reed could say anything.

He didn't stop. He kept them running toward the truck. "It'll be safer for you at Cooper's."

"We don't have a second to spare," Addison reminded him. "Those men are shooting at Emily."

Mercy, it broke her heart just to say that aloud, but Reed certainly couldn't dispute it. She wanted him there when Marshal Walker came through the gate, and for that to happen, they'd need to leave now and not waste the precious minutes it'd take for him to drop her off at Cooper's and then turn around to head to the back part of the ranch.

Reed was cursing when they jumped into the truck, but he didn't go toward Cooper's house. Thank God. He sped down the side dirt road that would lead them away from the main house.

"You'll need to stay inside the truck and keep down," he growled. He obviously wasn't happy about bringing her along, but like her, he knew what had to be done. "There's a gun in the glove compartment. Not that I want you to use it. I'm serious about that staying-down part. But I want you to have it just in case."

Just in case Reed and the ranch hands couldn't stop those men following the SUV. Even though Addison wasn't a good shot by any means, she did have some training. Most folks did in this rural part of Texas. And she wouldn't be afraid to use the gun if it meant protecting her baby.

The truck bobbled over the uneven road, and both Reed and she kept watch around them.

Not that there was much to see.

The ranch hands who were usually all over the grounds either had moved to the front fence or were on their way to the back to help Reed and her. She prayed that everyone got in place in time and then added a prayer that none of the bullets got anywhere near Emily.

"The marshals will protect the baby with their lives," Reed reminded her.

The reminder helped a little, but the only thing that would truly help was for this to be over and to have Emily safe in her arms. And to see the people responsible for this behind bars.

Just as he took one of the curves on the road, his phone rang, and Reed handed it to her so she could answer it.

"It's Colt," she relayed to Reed, and put the call on speaker.

"Is Emily all right?" Addison asked before Colt said anything.

"She's fine," Colt answered.

Whether that was true or not, she didn't know, but for her sanity Addison believed him.

"The gunmen in one of the cars disabled a marshal's vehicle that was trying to stop them," Colt continued, "but Marshal Walker got away and is headed for that gate at the back of the ranch."

If the attackers had managed to do that, then they could disable Walker's SUV, too.

"Darnell will open the gate," Reed said to him. "And I'll be there in a minute or two."

"Good. Cooper and I are both on the way."

"You need to make sure the front of the ranch is secure," Reed insisted. "This could all be a ploy to pull us away so these goons can come barreling onto the ranch. Right now there are probably only two hands to cover that whole wooded area where the shooters could hide out."

Colt paused a moment. He'd probably already considered that this could be some kind of trap, but like Reed and her, he was no doubt trying to figure out how to protect the others on the ranch, including Rosalie and her baby daughter.

"I'll go to the front of the ranch," Colt finally said. "When he gets there, Cooper can go to the back with Darnell and you."

"How soon before Marshal Walker reaches the gate?" Reed asked. Once he cleared another curve, she spotted the two old hay barns ahead.

"I'm estimating less than five minutes. Just make sure Darnell has the gate open."

Reed assured Colt that he would, and ended the call.

Addison had been on the Sweetwater Ranch plenty of times but never to this part of the grounds. Thankfully, there weren't a lot of trees, so that meant fewer places for gunmen to hide. However, it also meant there wasn't much cover for Reed and the ranch hands, either.

Reed slowed when he saw one of the ranch hands standing next to a truck that was parked near the barn. It was Quint Gifford, someone she knew well. He wasn't just a ranch hand but also an auxiliary cop who Cooper sometimes used in emergency situations.

"Is Darnell by the gate?" Reed asked, lowering the window.

Quint nodded and tipped his head to the road. "The gate's just around that curve there, and Darnell took Grange with him."

Addison knew Grange, too. He was another of Reed's ranch hands. Not an auxiliary cop like Quint, but he was still someone she trusted.

"Cell service is spotty out here," Quint continued, "so we all three have walkie-talkies if you need to get in touch with him."

So, only two ranch hands, but Addison reminded herself there were armed marshals in the SUV. Maybe that meant their attackers were outnumbered and would back off. She hated they couldn't just end the threat right here, right now, but Addison didn't want to do that until Emily was safely tucked away.

Reed pulled the truck off the road and to the side of the barn. "Wait here with Quint," he told her. He started toward the gate but then looked back over his shoulder. First at her. Then at Quint.

"If there's trouble," Reed added to the ranch hands, "make sure you get her out of the way."

Quint nodded, and while Addison didn't like the idea of anyone, including Quint, putting themselves on the line to protect her, she wouldn't argue, since she didn't want to delay Reed getting to the gate. However, if trouble came, there was no way she'd hide while she could do something—anything—to protect Emily.

Reed hurried away, and it didn't take long for him to disappear around the curve. Quint and she stayed by his truck, both watching and waiting. Both armed.

Addison tried to pick through the sounds of the cool spring breeze and the leaves rattling on the shrubs so she could try to hear Reed, the others or even the sound of the marshal's SUV.

But there was nothing.

Well, nothing except her heavy breathing and her own heartbeat crashing in her ears. It was impossible to make herself stay calm.

Quint's walkie-talkie made a slight crackling sound, and without taking his attention off the road, he pushed the button to answer.

"The SUV's just up the road," she heard Darnell say. "Once it's through, I'll close the gate. Reed wants you and Addison to follow the marshal's SUV in the truck to Cooper's house."

That plan sounded good except for the part about Reed and other two ranch hands not going to Cooper's house with them. They'd stay, of course, to deal with the gunmen.

That sure didn't help her raw nerves.

Addison reminded herself that Reed was a cop, but it didn't help, either. He was also her ex-husband. Emily's father. And the man she'd slept with just a little while ago. Not that she'd needed that to remind her how important Reed was to her, but the intimacy had certainly given her a jolt.

She couldn't lose him.

"I hear a car engine," Quint said, lifting his head.

It took Addison a moment, but she heard it, as well. Even though she couldn't see the SUV, it was clearly traveling at a fast speed. There was a squeal of brakes, then the sound of tires flinging up gravel from the road.

Was that the SUV?

Addison prayed that it was. She didn't have to wait long for confirmation. Almost immediately, the marshal's SUV came barreling around the curve directly toward the barns.

However, that wasn't the only sound.

The gunshots blasted through the air.

Chapter Seventeen

Everything happened at once. Walker's SUV came tearing past the gate, the tires kicking up a spray of dirt and rocks. The debris smacked into Reed and the ranch hands. There'd been no way to prevent it. Not at the speed the marshal was going. Reed felt the sting of a cut above his eye. Heard the two hands yelp out in pain.

Worse, the oversize black truck carrying the attackers sped in right behind the SUV. Right on its tail. There was no time for Reed to make a move to shut the gate.

The black truck came right toward them.

Reed jumped to the side, and in the same motion, he fired. Not at the gunmen, whose windows were all down. But at the tires. It took three shots, but he finally disabled the front passenger's tire.

Darnell took aim at the tires, too. Thank God it worked, because the truck wobbled to a stop.

"Take cover," Reed told Darnell and Grange.

Both ranch hands scrambled to the sides of some shrubs. Definitely not much protection, but at least the truck was no longer heading toward the SUV. Maybe Dallas could get Emily safely away from this, and while he was wishing, Reed added that there wouldn't be a second attack at the front of the ranch, since Colt likely hadn't had time to get there yet.

Reed braced himself for the men in the truck to come out with guns blazing. That didn't happen.

There was nothing but silence.

He couldn't even see inside. The back window was heavily tinted, but he thought he'd seen three men in the vehicle. Not bad odds. Reed figured he could take at least two of them out, leaving the third for Darnell and Grange.

Then Reed heard another sound.

One that put his heart right in his throat.

Movement. Not from the guys in the black truck, either. Someone was running from the road and onto the ranch grounds.

Hell.

If it was Cooper out there, he would have given Reed some kind of warning. No. This was almost certainly the attackers who'd been in that second vehicle. The ones who'd managed to disable the marshals' backup car that'd been following Walker to the safe house.

Reed couldn't see anyone, but there was no mistaking where those hurried footsteps were going.

Toward the barns where he'd left Addison.

"Tell Quint that danger's coming his way and to stop those men when they get out of the truck," Reed whispered to Darnell.

Yeah, it was a risk to leave the two ranch hands, but it was an even bigger risk to leave Addison, because she was almost certainly these goons' main target.

Reed started running, too. Not on the road by the truck. The men inside would just gun him down. Instead he ducked behind some shrubs and used them for cover. Not ideal. But maybe it would get him close enough to protect Addison.

Or not.

He'd barely made it a few steps when someone shot at him.

The blast was loud. Probably from a rifle. The bullet tore through the bushes just above his head. Reed scrunched down even lower, but he kept moving. Had to. No way could he let these killers get to Addison, especially since they'd had no trouble killing Cissy and leaving her sister for dead.

Another shot ripped through the shrubs, but even over the blast, Reed heard other shots. Behind him. No doubt coming from Darnell and Grange. Maybe from the other guys in the truck, too.

But there was more.

A shot farther up the road. Right in the direction of the barns.

That got Reed moving even faster, and he had to remind himself to stay low. It wouldn't do Addison and Quint any good if he got himself shot while trying to reach them.

Thankfully, the shrubs got thicker after he ran the next twenty yards. Reed used them and hoped like the devil he wasn't too late. There were way too many shots being fired, and by now any one of them could have hit Addison.

It seemed to take a couple of lifetimes, but Reed finally made it to the barns. And immediately didn't like what he saw. Addison was there, at the back corner of the nearest barn, and Quint had his gun drawn and was hovering over her.

For a good reason.

Those idiot attackers were shooting at them.

Addison lifted her head, her gaze snapping right to Reed, but he motioned for her to stay down. She did, and Reed glanced around trying to spot the gunmen.

He didn't see them, but judging from the angle of the shots, they were lying in the deep ditch across the dirt road from the barns.

Reed fired a shot at them and hurried those last few yards to Addison.

Her breath rushed out. She was obviously relieved to see him, but Reed knew there was nothing to be relieved about yet. Yeah, he'd made it to her, but there were plenty of would-be killers in the area. Those men back by the gate with the flat tires and heaven knew how many here.

"Dallas radioed Quint. He, Emily and the others made it to Cooper's house," Addison told him immediately.

That was great news. Now Reed had to make sure these gunmen didn't make it anywhere near Cooper's while he kept Addison safe.

But how?

There wasn't a back door to the barn and trying to reach the front would be suicide. Still, if they could get inside the barn, they'd have some cover, and he'd be in a better position to take out the shooters in the ditch.

"See if there are any loose boards," Reed said to Quint.

He heard Quint doing just that, but Reed couldn't help him. He didn't dare take his attention off their attackers. And he finally got lucky. One of them levered up, no doubt to get a better shot at Addison and them, but Reed took aim and fired first.

Reed's bullet slammed into the man's chest, causing him to crumple to the ground. Maybe he was dead. Or at least out of commission so Reed had a better chance of dealing with the ones still alive.

To his right, he heard Quint and Addison pulling at some of the boards. He also heard the gunmen scrambling around in the ditch. They were either helping their fallen comrade or getting in a better position to return fire.

Reed got a quick answer about that, too.

There were three of them, and he saw the tops of their heads when they fanned out over the ditch. It put the one on Reed's left in solid position to fire at him.

Something the man immediately did.

Reed pulled back behind the barn just as Quint and Addison managed to rip off several boards. It wasn't a huge space, but it was big enough for them to get inside.

"Check and make sure no one else is in there," Reed warned Quint.

The ranch hand's eyes widened because he obviously hadn't thought they could be ambushed inside. But it was possible. Their attackers could have managed to get someone inside the barn before the ranch hands even arrived.

Hell, there could be gunmen scattered all over the ranch.

Not exactly a thought to tamp down the adrenaline knifing through him.

"I think it's empty," Quint finally said.

Think. In other words, he couldn't be certain. Reed hadn't been in these particular barns in years, but he figured there was still some hay. Maybe ranch equipment, too.

Plenty of places for killers to hide.

Still, he didn't have a lot of options. With the new position of the gunmen in the ditch, the shots started coming at them, and Reed had to do something to stop this in case all of these bullets were simply a ruse so that one of the goons could get closer to Addison.

Or God forbid Emily.

"Crawl through," Reed said to Addison.

She still had hold of the gun, and while it took some maneuvering, she got through the ragged opening with Reed following right behind her.

Even though there was plenty of sunshine outside, not much was making its way into the barn. Just threads of light spearing through the spaces between the boards. It created an eerie effect, but worse, it made it hard for him to tell if someone was in there hiding.

Reed had been right about the huge number of hiding spots in the sprawling space. Hay bales were stacked above his head in spots, and there was a tractor and a small bulldozer near the front.

Outside and up the road, Reed heard another shot. Not near the houses. This one had come from the area near the first barn where he'd left Darnell. Maybe Darnell had managed to take out one of the hired guns.

"Keep watch behind us," Reed said to Quint. He put Addison between them and made his way to the front door.

Reed motioned for Addison to drop down next to the tractor. It wasn't much protection, but at least it had enough metal on it that it could be used to stop a bullet or two. He eased open the front door, ready to take aim at the gunmen in the ditch.

But taking aim was as far as he got.

The shot blasted through the air. However, Reed immediately knew this was no ordinary shot.

A split second later, he got that confirmed the hard way.

The metal canister bashed through the wood on the front of the barn and clanged to the floor just a few yards behind Addison, Quint and him.

Tear gas began to spew throughout the barn.

BEFORE ADDISON EVEN realized what was happening, her eyes started to burn, and her breath clogged in her throat.

"Tear gas," Reed managed to say, and he latched on to Addison's hand and got her running away from the canister and toward the back of the barn.

Oh, mercy.

There was only one reason their attackers would use something like that—to get them out in the open again.

Something that would definitely have to happen.

None of them could breathe and were coughing nonstop. It only got worse when a second canister came flying into the barn and more of the gas hissed out and around them.

With Quint right behind her, Reed kept her moving, and they finally reached the opening they'd made at the back. Addison instincts were to hurry through it so she could gulp in her fresh air, but Reed held her back.

Without Reed at the front of the barn to fire shots at them, those gunmen could have hurried to the back so they'd be in place to attack them.

Still coughing, Reed peered out. No doubt looking for those men. And he must not have seen them, because he motioned for Quint and her to hurry out.

They did.

Addison dragged in several much-needed breaths, but her eyes were still on fire. She couldn't see much of anything. However, Reed must have been able to see, because he kept her moving.

"We can't stay out in the open," Reed said through the coughs.

He'd no sooner spoken those words than another shot was fired. Not from the front of the barn, either. This one had come from the side.

The gunmen were coming for them.

Reed positioned himself in front of her. Protecting her. Quint tried to do the same, and the second they reached the second barn, they immediately started to bash through the back of it, as well.

More shots came.

They flew into the old barn, shattering the wood.

Reed stopped kicking in the boards so he could take aim at the men. He fired. The shot was so close that it clanged in her ears. Even if someone had been standing right in front of her, Addison doubted she would be able to see or hear him now.

Thankfully, that didn't seem to be Reed's problem. He sent another shot toward the gunmen. No doubt to buy them some time to get through the boards.

And that was exactly what it did.

In those few precious seconds, they loosened enough of the wood so that Quint could shimmy inside. As he'd done before, he looked around, his gun ready, and motioned for her to come in. He didn't have to make the offer twice. Addison crawled in through the ragged opening, scraping herself along the way, and pulled in Reed after her.

"Make sure no one's here," Reed said to Quint.

The ranch hand went to do just that while Reed stayed at the back opening. He took aim at something and fired. At first, Addison thought it was just another shot to keep the gunmen at bay, but he leaned out and fired one more shot.

"Got him," Reed said. "I think there's only one of them left. One here anyway."

That sent another wave of fear through her. She wasn't sure what exactly had gone on at the gate, but judging from the sounds she'd heard, there'd been a second vehicle. One that Reed, Darnell and Grange had managed to stop because it hadn't come past the barns.

However, it didn't mean they had stopped the men inside that vehicle.

Sweet heaven. How many of them were out here?

And were any of them trying to get to Emily?

These monsters had to know that if they managed to grab Emily that Reed and she would do anything to get the baby back. And in Addison's case, *anything* meant she'd exchange herself for Emily.

Since a full-blown panic attack wasn't going to help anyone, Addison tried to tamp down her wild thoughts. Not easy to do with her baby less than a mile away. But she had to believe Reed when he said that Marshal Walker and the others would protect Emily with their lives.

Maybe it wouldn't come down to that.

"See anything?" Reed asked Quint.

Again, the ranch hand shook his head, but he continued to look around the barn. So did Reed, but he stayed toward the back, volleying his attention between there and the barn's front door.

Now that her eyes had cleared a little, Addison was able to take a look around, too. Like in the other barn, there were some hay bales. Sacks of feed, as well. And seemingly dozens of shadowy places for one of those gunmen to hide. It didn't help that the front door was open and creaking with each gust of wind.

Addison tried to calm her own heartbeat so she could listen for any sounds that shouldn't be there. Hard to do, though, when everything inside her was racing. The fear had her by the throat, but she fought it and kept looking.

Another gust of wind caught the door, the rusty

hinges squealing, but the flash of light from the opening allowed her to see some of the corners.

Empty.

Well, unless someone had crouched down. But if one of the gunmen had been waiting inside for them, then why hadn't he just shot them when they first stepped inside?

Or fired another tear gas canister in the barn?

If that happened, then Reed, Quint and she would have no place to go. There weren't enough trees and shrubs nearby to use for cover.

Unless they made it to the truck.

Yes, it was a risk, but anything they did at this point would be. They could maybe use the truck to draw the rest of the gunmen far away from Emily.

Of course, Reed might have plenty to say about that idea. He was the good guy, the lawman, and his instincts would be to get her to safety so he could take on these killers without her.

The door creaked again, and like before, Addison used the opportunity to look around. This time, in the hayloft that was a good fifteen feet above them. Maybe it was her watery eyes playing tricks on her, but Addison thought she saw something.

Or rather some*one*.

Who was up there?

"Reed," she said, and motioned toward the loft. She hurried behind one of the hay bale stacks just in case.

That got Reed's immediate attention, and he stood so he could see where she was pointing. But the light was already gone, and even though her eyes had adjusted some to the darkness, she still couldn't tell if there was anyone in the loft or if her mind was playing tricks on her.

Addison soon got her answer.

"Get down!" Reed shouted.

She ducked lower next to the hay bales.

But she wasn't fast enough.

Reed took aim at the loft. Fired. However, whoever was up there got off a shot first.

The pain was instant as something sliced into her arm.

Chapter Eighteen

Reed cursed, fired a shot at the guy in the hayloft and then raced toward Addison. He caught her before she fell to the floor.

She'd been shot.

At least that was his first thought, but he fought through the panic and realized that hadn't been the sound of a gun being fired. Not an ordinary one anyway. When he pushed her hand away from her arm, he realized exactly what'd happened.

Someone had shot her with a tranquilizer gun.

"Are you all right?" Reed asked, still watching the loft. Whoever had fired had already moved back into the shadows so that Reed could no longer see him.

"It stings," Addison said, already sounding woozy.

Still cursing, Reed pulled the small dart from her arm. It probably wasn't poison—that wouldn't make sense. If their attacker wanted her dead, he could have just shot her with a bullet. So someone wanted her sedated.

And the question was why?

The only thing Reed could come up with was that someone wanted her alive so they could question her about what she'd learned from Cissy, and that someone no doubt wanted to try to kidnap her again.

"You see who fired that dart?" Quint whispered from the stack of feed sacks where he'd taken cover.

"No."

But he still had to be there. Waiting. Probably for Addison to lose consciousness.

Something that might happen soon.

Even though he couldn't see it clearly, he tried to look at the spot where the dart had hit her. It appeared to have gone partly into the seam of her top, by her shoulder.

Partly.

Of course, the other part was in her, and that meant she needed medical attention.

Reed spotted an old hammer on the floor of the barn. He picked it up and tossed it into the loft. He couldn't see exactly where it landed, but it must have gotten close enough to the dart shooter for him to come out of cover.

Big mistake.

Reed double-tapped the trigger and took him out. Well, hopefully. The guy fell back anyway, and Reed didn't want to waste time going up there to find out if he was still alive. For now, just having him out of commission would do. Of course, he'd have to keep watch to make sure the moron didn't try to fire another one of those darts.

"Keep an eye on the hayloft," Reed told Quint.

While Reed did the same, he took out his phone and fired off a text to Colt. He kept it short but let Colt know that they needed an ambulance and that he was going to try to get Addison out to his truck.

"Emily," Addison said, licking her lips. "Ask Colt how she is."

Well, at least Addison was alert enough to realize what was going on. That was good. Maybe Colt would have equally good news on that front.

Reed eased Addison onto the floor. "Stay here a second," he whispered to her, and hoped that she did.

The last time he'd seen their attacker outside, the guy had been in the back of the barn. Too close to the gaping hole that Addison, Quint and he had created so they could get inside. Keeping low, Reed went there first and dragged a couple of hay bales in front of it. That wouldn't stop a gunman, but it might slow him down enough so this flimsy plan of Reed's might work.

"Check and see if anyone's out front," Reed told Quint.

The ranch hand crept his way there and peered out the door. Several moments later, he shook his head. "I don't see anyone."

That was a start. "Stay here with Addison," Reed insisted, keeping his voice as low as possible.

"No, don't leave me." She caught on to his arm. Or rather tried, but her grip was too weak for her to hold on.

"I won't be long." Reed brushed a kiss on her cheek and hoped it would help soothe her nerves. It sure helped his a little.

Quint scooted in next to Addison, and that was Reed's cue to get himself moving.

"If that idiot in the loft is still alive and moves a fraction, shoot him," he told Quint. "I'm getting the truck. Stay away from the door, because I'm bringing the truck in here."

Quint made a sound of surprise. Maybe even disbelief. Yeah, it was definitely a flimsy plan. But it was the only one Reed had at the moment.

Reed used the feed sacks and hay for cover while he made his way to the front door. No one in sight, just as Quint had said. He took a deep breath, readied his gun and raced out toward the truck. He braced himself for gunfire.

It didn't come.

And that unnerved him even more than if it had.

He got into the truck as fast as he could, and once he started the engine, he lined up the front end with the door. The barn door was plenty wide enough to get the truck through, but fully opening it would have required pulling it back and anchoring the latch.

No time for that.

Reed threw the truck in gear and crashed through the barn. Before he even came to a full stop, he leaned over, threw open the passenger's door and motioned for Quint to get Addison inside. However, Reed's phone rang just as Quint scooped her up in his arms.

"We got another problem," Colt said the moment Reed answered. Reed put the phone on the dash so he could free up his hands to help Quint get Addison onto the seat.

"Yeah, Addison needs an ambulance," Reed said immediately.

"It's on the way, but we've got an even bigger problem. Darnell and Grange managed to get one of the gunmen alive. And he's talking. Or rather bragging. Reed, there's someone in the barn with you."

"I know. He was in the hayloft, and I shot him."

"No. According to this gunman, there's somebody else. Their boss is in the barn with you," Colt added quickly. "They sneaked onto the ranch before all of us even got out here."

Reed hadn't needed any other reasons to hurry, but that did it. Colt's news also caused his heart to slam against his chest. If the person responsible for this was truly inside, he wanted to face him down, badly, but he didn't want to do that with Addison next to him.

But Reed would definitely come back for him.

He threw the truck into Reverse, ready to barrel out of there. However, Reed didn't make it far before the blast tore through the barn.

EVERYTHING WAS SWIMMING in and out of focus, but even with her blurry head and eyes, Addison had no trouble hearing the explosion. It was deafening, and it ripped through the front of the barn. Hay, bits of wood and other debris rained down on them.

"Get on the floor of the truck," Reed told her.

Addison immediately tried to do just that, but her arms and legs didn't want to cooperate. What had been in the little dart that'd slammed into her arm? Whatever it was, it had made her drowsy.

Quint helped her. He caught on to her shoulder and pushed her to the floor, but the new position didn't stop her from hearing another sound.

A bad one.

This time, it was a gunshot, and it slammed into the front of the truck. It was quickly followed by another. Then another.

Soon, they were in a hail of gunfire.

"He's shooting out the engine," Reed snarled, and hit the accelerator, no doubt ready to get them out of there by crashing through the barn's back wall.

But that didn't happen.

Not only was the front entrance blocked from the debris of the explosion, but the truck engine clanged to a stop. The gunman has managed to disable the engine after all, leaving them sitting ducks.

"Step out with your hands up," someone shouted.

It wasn't a voice that she recognized, but it seemed to be coming from the far right corner of the barn. One of the gunmen, no doubt.

"Stay down," Reed told her.

He'd no sooner said that than another shot bashed into the truck. This one crashed through the front windshield. If she'd still been on the seat, it would have gone right into her.

"I've got dozens of bullets," their attacker added. "And if you don't get out of the truck now, I'll keep firing until you're all dead."

Addison had known right from the start that the man didn't have friendly intentions, but it sickened her to have it spelled out like this. Quint and Reed could die because these monsters wanted her.

And she still didn't know why.

What was it that they believed Cissy had told her?

"What should we do?" Quint asked Reed.

Despite her blurry vision, she saw the muscles flicker in Reed's jaw. "I'll get out. Try to cover me as best you can, and I'll pretend to surrender to see if I can eliminate this guy."

"No." Addison took hold of his arm to try to stop him. "If you go out there, he'll just shoot you. We can maybe hold out until backup gets here."

Reed's gaze met hers for just a split second. "It's too dangerous for backup. I need to put an end to this and hope that Darnell and Colt can take care of the others out there."

Maybe it was the drug, but it felt as if her heart skipped a beat or two.

The others.

Yes, there probably were more out there. More who might go after Emily. As much as it sickened her to have

Reed in danger, Addison knew he didn't have a choice. They had to protect the baby, and the first step was stopping the immediate threat of the shooter.

Reed kept his gun in his hand, but he did lift his arms in surrender when he stepped out of the truck.

"What do you want?" he shouted to their attacker.

They didn't have to wait long for an answer. "I want Addison and the other guy. Tell them to get out, too."

"You drugged Addison. She can't even stand up."

"Then have her lean on you. Just get her out of the truck, or I start shooting again. You'll be the first to die, Deputy."

There was no way she could stay put after hearing that. Because Addison knew in her gut that this man wasn't bluffing. He'd kill Reed on the spot. Quint, too. And then he'd take her to get whatever information it was they wanted from her.

Even though it was an effort, Addison got moving. Quint tried to hold her back, but she shoved his hand away and practically tumbled out of the driver's-side door. If Reed hadn't caught her, she would have dropped right onto the barn floor.

Thankfully, she managed to keep hold of her gun, and she positioned it by her side. Maybe they'd get lucky, and their attacker wouldn't see it.

"Satisfied?" she managed to snap.

But clearly Reed wasn't satisfied with what she'd done. He aimed a split-second scowl at her that even her in-and-out vision didn't have any trouble interpreting.

"It was the only way," she whispered to Reed. Addison pulled in a long breath so she could start trying to work out a deal with the person on the other end of that gun. "I'm here. Now tell me what you want."

"First, I want the other man out of the truck. He

needs to put down his gun and lie on the floor. The deputy has to toss his gun, too."

Even though Addison would have liked for Quint to be able to hold on to his gun, she couldn't risk him being killed. She motioned for him to do as the man said, but Quint refused to move until he got a nod from Reed.

While Quint was getting down on the floor, Addison nudged Reed with her gun so that he'd know she had it. He tossed his own weapon to the floor and then took hers, keeping it hidden between them.

"Now, what the hell do you want?" Reed repeated. He also inched his way in front of her so he could no doubt try to protect her.

"I want Addison, of course," someone said.

Not the other man who'd been ordering them around. This was definitely a voice she recognized. Her entire body knotted because she seriously doubted he'd been kidnapped and brought here.

No.

He was here because he was the man who wanted her dead.

Chapter Nineteen

"Why are you doing this?" Addison asked the man.

Dominic.

Addison's lawyer, a man she'd trusted. In the beginning anyway. Reed figured that her one-word question covered a multitude of sins.

"Because I need to find out what Cissy and Mellie told you," Dominic readily volunteered. "I also need to know what that fake P.I. learned."

Dominic's voice was eerily calm, as was his expression. An expression that Reed soon got to see because the lawyer stepped from the shadows as if he'd been on a leisurely stroll rather than behind a killing spree. However, the man was armed. Ditto for the two goons who stepped out with him.

Hell.

Three of them. And there might even be others hiding and ready to come to their boss's aid.

"See if the other situations are under control so we can leave," Dominic said to one of the men. The guy dropped back a step and started whispering into a small communicator clipped to his collar.

Situations. Reed didn't know what that all entailed, but he figured he wasn't going to like any of it. Especially if it involved Emily.

"What kind of drug did you use on Addison?" Reed demanded. And he prayed it wasn't something that would do permanent damage.

Or worse.

"She'll be okay," Dominic answered. Which wasn't much of an answer at all. "For now."

Reed didn't intend to trust anything this nut job said, but he had to figure a way out of this. He had the gun he'd gotten from Addison, so maybe he'd get a chance to use it on Dominic and his henchmen, but he couldn't just start firing, because those gunmen would be able to kill Addison and Quint.

"Cissy and Mellie didn't tell me anything," Addison insisted.

Unlike with Dominic, there was plenty of emotion in her voice, and she was shaking. Maybe from the drugs that Dominic's hired gun had shot into her, but it was also likely from the fear. They were literally facing down a killer.

"Right," Dominic grumbled, clearly not convinced Addison was telling the truth.

"What could Cissy and Mellie have possibly told Addison that would make her your target?" Reed demanded.

But that only earned him a lifted eyebrow from Dominic.

So Reed decided to spell out his theory as to why Dominic was here. "You probably lured Cissy and Mellie into your black market baby scheme. Along with countless others, including ones that you got from Quarles's youth group. Was Quarles in on it? Or maybe Cantor? Did one of them put this together?"

"Please. Cantor only got in the way. And Quarles? Well, I don't need that idiot judge's help," Dominic snarled. "He was born into money. Never made a dime of it on his own."

"Unlike you," Addison fired back. She was suddenly sounding a lot less woozy. And riled to the core for a darn good reason. Dominic had repeatedly put Emily and them in danger.

Reed hoped that Colt and the others would arrive soon so he'd have some backup, something he'd need to get Addison out of there. In the meantime, Reed would uncover more information that he could use to hang this guy.

"If Quarles or Cantor didn't help, then why did it look as if they were involved?" Reed asked.

"Because that's the way I wanted it to look. Cantor was easy with those sad puppy dog eyes looking for Cissy. All those big brother feelings for her. He made an easy mark because he was too wrapped up in finding her that he forgot to keep watch over his shoulder."

And Dominic had taken full advantage of that. Well, at least they weren't dealing with more than one slime bag boss here. The responsibility was solely Dominic's.

"You wormed your way into my life," Addison said, "so you could find out what I knew."

"Of course," Dominic admitted.

"You must have fathered Mellie's baby, too. Why else would you have stolen the DNA sample?" Reed tossed out there.

Dominic didn't confirm it, not with words anyway, but his expression said that was exactly what'd happened. "You shouldn't have hired the fake P.I.," he insisted, his glare aimed at Addison.

Yeah, because that was what had spooked Dominic. It might have spooked him even more when he'd learned that P.I. was a fake, because Cantor had personal reasons for wanting to protect Cissy and Mellie.

Dominic glanced at his hired gun, who was still whispering into the communicator, but the guy just held up his hand in a *still working on it* gesture. Maybe the hired guns were having trouble containing the *situations*.

Good.

"You killed Cissy and then tried to do the same to Mellie," Addison snapped.

"I *will* do the same to Mellie," Dominic corrected. "She can't stay alive. She knows too much."

Reed wished he could call the hospital and warn Pete, who was guarding Mellie. Maybe Dominic hadn't sent anyone else yet to finish the job.

"You murdered Cissy in cold blood," Addison added. She moved as if to step in front of Reed, but he got right back in front of her.

Dominic shook his head, and for the first time during this sick meeting, he looked remorseful. Or something. "That was a mistake. I actually…had feelings for Cissy."

"Right," Reed repeated, tossing Dominic's own skeptical response right back in his face.

Another headshake. "Cissy let it slip that she wanted to talk to Addison so she could reassure her that the surrogacy was legal and that Emily was indeed Addison's kid. I told her that the DNA tests would prove that, but she said she'd already written Addison a letter and wanted to talk to her…" His words trailed off.

"So you lost your temper and killed her," Reed finished for him. "Then you put her body in Addison's house as some kind of sick warning."

"Cissy's and Mellie's babies won't be hurt," Dominic said as if that excused all the murders and his other crimes. "I'll need to have them taken out of the country, of course. Can't have their DNA linked back to me."

It turned Reed's stomach to see how recklessly Dominic was playing with people's lives, including babies'. His own daughter had gotten caught up in Dominic's plan to cover up the truth.

"And I'm another loose end," Addison said. "You plan to kill me."

Dominic glanced at his chatting hired gun again, and the guy came over and whispered something in Dominic's ear. Something that clearly didn't please the lawyer.

"I won't kill you until I find out who else you might have told about the baby farm," Dominic said, turning his attention back to Addison.

"I told no one," she practically shouted.

Dominic lifted his shoulder. "If you didn't, then let me apologize. It won't save your life. Or theirs," he added, tipping his head to Reed and Quint. "But at least know that I'm sorry for the overkill."

It took everything inside Reed to stay back and not launch himself at this piece of scum. Dominic was treating this with no more emotion than carrying out the trash.

"Reed?" someone called out.

Colt.

With the tip of Dominic's head, one of the gunmen hurried toward the back of the barn. The other moved to the front. Maybe Colt wouldn't just go in there with guns blazing, but Reed couldn't stand by and do nothing, either. These men would kill Colt without blinking an eye.

"If you tell the deputy who's in here," Dominic said to Reed, "then you'll be signing his death warrant, too."

Yeah, but that didn't mean Reed couldn't do something else to warn him. "Stay back, Colt!" Reed shouted.

A flash of anger went through Dominic's eyes. Cold and calculating. And just as quickly, Dominic took aim at the one person in the barn who would definitely get Reed to stand down.

Addison.

Dominic aimed his weapon right at her head. "I said I wanted to talk to her first, but if you press the situation, she dies now."

The guy was clearly a sociopath, and Reed got a glimpse of the intense rage that Dominic must have unleashed on Cissy when the young woman had admitted she'd written that letter to Addison.

"We have another problem," Colt shouted back to him. "Whoever's behind this has taken a hostage."

THE EFFECTS OF the drug were already wearing off, but that helped to instantly clear Addison's head.

Oh, God.

"Emily!" she shouted, and would have bolted from the barn if Reed hadn't taken hold of her.

"It's not Emily," Dominic said. He still had that gun aimed at her and motioned for her to stay put. "It's Mellie."

Even though that was horrible news, Addison still felt some relief. It wasn't her baby in immediate danger, but it was an innocent woman.

"What about Pete, the deputy?" Reed asked.

"He's still with Mellie, and they'll stay safe as long as Addison comes with me."

Addison's shoulders snapped back. "Pete has no idea you're behind this. You have no reason to hurt him."

Partly a lie. Pete did know that Dominic was a suspect in the kidnapping attempts and Cissy's murder, but the deputy had no way of knowing that it was Dominic holding Reed, Quint and her at gunpoint right now.

"Then don't let Pete become a casualty in something you can stop," Dominic warned her.

"Addison's not going with you," Reed said before she could respond.

She shook her head. "But Pete and Mellie..."

Reed kept his attention pinned to Dominic, and because his hand was against her leg, she felt his grip tighten on the gun. "Dominic plans to kill them anyway."

Addison wanted to believe Pete might be spared, but Reed was right.

Dominic had already admitted that Mellie would have to die, so why wouldn't he just do the same to Pete? Her former lawyer was trying to tie up loose ends, and that might include not just Pete but anyone who'd had access to the investigation.

"You were the person behind the baby farms," Addison blurted out.

"I've already closed down the last of them," Dominic said, barely glancing at Addison before returning his gaze to Reed. "And I'm leaving the country. All you have to do to save lives is for you and Addison to come with me so we can have a little chat."

A chat that would no doubt involve some kind of torture in the hopes she'd rat out anyone who had a clue that Dominic was behind this.

"How do I know for sure the baby farms are closed?" Reed asked. He moved, just a fraction, placing himself even more in front of her than he already was. He was obviously getting ready to do something.

But what?

And better yet, how could she help him?

Quint was on the other side of the truck. Unarmed and an easy target for Dominic or his henchmen. If Reed lifted his gun and started shooting, Quint could die, since he might not even be able to get to cover. It was the same for Colt. Yes, Colt probably knew there were gunmen inside, but he might not realize that one of them had a gun trained on him.

"Once I'm out of the country," Dominic said to Reed, "I'll send the sheriff the locations of the now-closed baby farms. He can inspect them and see for himself that the operation is over."

"It's over now that you've made a ton of money and have killed countless people," Addison spat out. "And the babies. God knows where some of them have ended up."

She wasn't a violent person, but she wished she could stop Dominic right here, right now with some of those bullets that he'd used so freely.

Addison hadn't expected her comment to get a rise out of Dominic, but his gaze slashed from Reed to her. Maybe just the distraction they needed, so Addison tried to push even harder.

"Doesn't it bother you that your own babies were involved in this?" Addison didn't wait for Dominic to answer. "Did you sell them, too, like you did all those other newborns?"

Now that there was a huge gaping hole in the front of the barn, she had no trouble seeing the muscles flicker in Dominic's jaw. "That couldn't be helped. Cissy and Mellie aren't in positions to raise children, and I'm not ready to be a dad. I made sure they were placed in decent families."

Probably a good thing that the children had been adopted. Well, if he was telling the truth.

"Families who paid you thousands for babies you fathered with troubled young women that you used and discarded," Addison corrected.

"You need to send the sheriff records of all the adoptions, too," Reed insisted. "So he can make sure all the babies, not just your own, ended up in good homes. Or if you bothered to leave any of the other birth mothers alive, maybe Cooper can reunite them with their children. It'll take a lot to undo all the misery you've caused."

"Enough of this!" Dominic yelled. His jaw muscles didn't just flicker. They turned to stone. "Get in the truck now."

That must have been the cue the gunman at the front of the barn needed, because he motioned to someone outside. No doubt another hired killer. And he hurried to the truck. The doors were already open, and he motioned for Addison to get in.

This was it. What could be Reed's and Quint's last moments alive. At least it would be if Dominic got his way.

But Addison had no intention of letting this monster win.

She didn't have a weapon, or anything she could use to hurl at him, but she could still try to fight him with her bare hands. Reed must have sensed she was ready to do something, because he gave her a split-second glance.

"Get under the truck," he said to her.

Addison immediately dropped to the ground just as the shot cracked through the air.

"GET DOWN!" REED shouted to Quint, and he hoped the ranch hand did exactly that—and fast.

Thankfully, Addison scrambled as far beneath the truck as she could. It wasn't a second too soon, because the bullets started coming right toward them. Not just from Dominic but also from his two hired goons. All three men took cover behind the bulldozer and hay bales.

The shots blasted into the truck, and Reed had no choice but to drop down, as well. It wouldn't help Addison if he got himself killed.

"Reed?" Colt called out.

Judging from the sound of his voice, Colt was still at the back of the barn and no doubt armed, but if he came in shooting, he could be gunned down.

"Plenty of backup is on the way," Colt added.

Even over the gunfire, Reed heard Dominic cursing.

Good.

That meant the man hadn't planned for this. Well, hopefully not anyway. Dominic had probably figured he would have Addison in the truck and out of there by now.

"Watch out, Reed!" Quint yelled. "He's coming your way."

Reed's gaze swung to his right just in time to see the gunman at the back end of the truck. The guy was taking aim.

So did Reed.

And Reed pulled the trigger first.

The gunman wasn't wearing Kevlar, and the bullet smacked him right in the chest. He dropped like a stone to the ground.

One down, two to go.

But there was one Reed wanted more than the other.

Dominic. Because of that bastard, he'd nearly lost Addison and Emily, and Dominic would pay and pay hard for that.

Reed felt the movement at his feet and realized that Addison was throwing bits of the wooden debris out at Dominic and the other gunman. No doubt to distract them and get their attention off him. It wasn't the safest thing for her to do, but at this point nothing was safe.

The gunman at the rear of his truck appeared to be dead so Reed headed in that direction, scooping up the guy's weapon. He didn't have a lot of ammo and might need it if this fight went on much longer.

The moment he was at the other end of the truck, Reed spotted Quint. The ranch hand had taken cover behind the massive back tractor wheel. Dominic's gunman was shooting at him, but the bullets weren't going through the thick tire.

Dominic, however, was behind the bulldozer, and he was firing toward the bottom of the truck.

At Addison.

Hell. Reed had welcomed the distraction that she was creating, but she was going to get shot if she kept it up. Worse, Dominic was positioned behind the bulldozer, so Reed didn't have a shot to stop him.

"Dominic!" Reed shouted to get the man's attention off Addison.

It worked.

Dominic snapped toward Reed, and in the same motion, he fired.

Reed barely got out of the way in time, and the bullet tore off a chunk of the truck. Pieces of jagged metal flew through the air, some of them slicing into Reed's clothes and skin.

That didn't stop him.

Even though Dominic was still behind cover for the most part, Reed started shooting. Just as Dominic's bullet had done to the truck, Reed's did the same with the bulldozer. Bits of metal broke off, flinging into Dominic. One sliced across his cheek, causing the man to stagger back enough.

Just enough.

Dominic realized he was away from cover, and he lifted his gun toward Reed. But Reed was ready, and he fired right into the man's chest. Dominic froze, his startled gaze looking down at his wounded chest before he sank to his knees.

But that wasn't all he did.

Despite the shock and pain from being shot, Dominic turned his gun toward Reed and fired. Reed dropped.

Fired again.

Two more shots that went squarely into Dominic.

This time, Dominic didn't fire. He couldn't. There were no startled looks. No more anything.

Dominic fell, his gun clattering out of his hand when it hit the ground.

Almost immediately Colt came rushing through the hole in the back of the barn wall, and he pointed his gun at the other man. "Drop your weapon!" Colt ordered.

He didn't. Not at first anyway. But then he looked around at Reed and Quint and realized he didn't stand a chance. Cursing, he tossed his gun and lifted his hands in surrender.

"Are you okay?" Reed asked, ducking so he could see Addison.

She was terrified, but she didn't seem to be injured. Somewhat of a miracle with all those bullets flying around. Addison crawled out toward him, and the moment she reached the side of the truck, Reed pulled her to her feet and to him.

The relief was instant and so strong that it slammed hard into him. Addison was alive. And in his arms. So he kissed her. Yeah, the timing sucked, but Reed thought maybe she needed it as much as he did.

"Dominic's dead," Colt said.

Even though he'd been kissing Addison, Reed had kept an eye on both the gunman and Dominic. He'd figured the man was dead, and while he wasn't all torn up about that, Reed would have liked some answers.

"Maybe we can get info about the baby farms when we go through his office," Reed said.

"You won't find anything there," his hired gun said. He waited until he had Colt's and Reed's attention before he continued. "I want a plea deal, one with no jail time, and in exchange I'll tell you the location of every file that has anything to do with the baby operation."

"Right." Reed stared at him. "Any reason we should believe you?"

"Yeah," the guy snapped. "Because I'm about to give you something you really want."

"And what would that be?" Reed asked.

"Dominic had a backup plan. One that involved taking your daughter. Before we ever came into the barn, he sent a team to carry out that plan."

Addison gasped and latched on to the man's shirt. "What do you mean?" she demanded.

Dominic's hired gun tipped his head toward the ranch houses. "If you hurry, you can stop the baby from being kidnapped."

Chapter Twenty

It felt as if someone had knocked the breath right out of Reed. This couldn't be happening. Not now, after they'd already been through so much.

"You're lying," Reed said to the gunman.

But he knew he wasn't. There was something in the man's cold, dark eyes. A warning for Reed to hurry.

So that was what he did.

Addison hurried to Colt's truck, too, all the while mumbling a prayer. Reed was right there with her. Praying and determined to do whatever it took. He wouldn't lose his little girl.

"I'm calling Cooper!" Colt shouted out to Reed as they sped away.

Good. He'd take all the help he could get right now.

"Emily's well guarded," Reed reminded Addison. Reminded himself, too. She was with Marshal Walker, Cooper and the others, and they wouldn't let Dominic's hired goons just walk in and take her.

Of course, if there as a gunfight, Emily and everyone else could be right back in danger, as well.

So Reed hurried. Driving way too fast and yet it didn't seem nearly fast enough. The seconds just crawled by.

"Colt's probably already done it, but call Rosalie,"

he told Addison. "Just in case these kidnappers go to the main house instead of Cooper's."

"Oh, God," Addison mumbled.

She snatched up his phone and made the call. The fear practically dripped from her voice. Fear not just for Emily but for Rosalie and her baby, too.

"Rosalie said the doors were all locked and they're keeping watch," Addison relayed to him when she finished the call.

Reed hoped that would be enough.

He didn't see any sign of trouble when he drove past the main house and guest cottage. There were still ranch hands guarding the front of the property, where they'd been for the last half hour or so.

"How would Dominic have managed to get his men onto this part of the grounds?" Addison asked, her gaze also going to the ranch hands. They weren't just covering the wooded area; they were on the road that led to the ranch.

Sadly, Reed knew a way Dominic could have done it. "He could have already had his men in place before this latest attack."

No one could just come driving up unnoticed to the ranch, but with all the activity that'd been going on, it was possible for someone to come in on foot. For that matter, Dominic could have sneaked the men in the night before so they'd be in place, waiting and ready to strike.

Reed slowed as they approached Cooper's sprawling house. Again, nothing seemed out of place, and he spotted the marshal's SUV parked out front in the circular drive. There certainly wasn't a fight in progress.

But then he spotted someone.

"Get down," he told Addison, something he'd had to do way too much lately. But again, it was necessary.

Because he saw a man dressed in dark clothes at the back of the house. The guy was peering into one of the windows but stopped when the sound of the truck engine caught his attention.

The man turned, lifted his gun and fired at Reed.

The shot tore through the windshield, shattering it, and it made it impossible to see out. Reed gave the steering wheel a sharp turn to the right, turning the truck so that he could see through the side window. It was already down, so Reed took aim.

Careful aim.

He didn't want the shot going into the house.

Reed's bullet smacked into his shoulder. It wasn't enough to kill him, but it did cause him to drop his gun. Probably because at the exact moment, Cooper came storming out the back door. The sheriff was armed and clearly not happy that someone was stupid enough to attack anyone inside his own home.

With Cooper arresting the injured gunman, Reed fired glances around for more. The deal-pleading gunman in the barn had said Dominic had sent in a pair.

"There's another one," Reed called out to Cooper.

Cooper nodded. "Marshal Walker got him right after Colt called." He pushed the injured gunman against the house and used a pair of plastic cuffs to keep him restrained.

"Emily?" Addison said, and before Reed could stop her, she barreled out of the truck.

Reed went after her, just in case all was not well, and he glanced over at Cooper, who was restraining the injured gunman with plastic cuffs. Hopefully, Dallas was doing the same thing to the other one. If the guy was still alive, that is.

Addison made it to the porch ahead of Reed, but he stopped her at the door, just in case Dominic had sent in more than a pair of kidnappers. However, the door flew open, and there were no kidnappers inside.

But there were guns.

Both of the other marshals had pulled their weapons, ready to protect Emily. However, the baby was nowhere in sight.

"Emily?" Addison called out.

"She's in the bathroom just off the hall," one of the marshals told her.

Reed and Addison ran in that direction, but the two other marshals stayed in place, no doubt to make sure the attack was truly over.

"It's us, Emily's parents," Reed said when they reached the hall bathroom, just in case the bodyguard-nanny was armed and ready to shoot whoever tried to get in.

The woman eased open the door. Yeah, she was armed all right, but she wasn't holding Emily. That caused his heart to slam against his chest. Until Reed saw Emily in her infant seat, which had been positioned in the empty bathtub. A safety precaution, since bullets couldn't go through the porcelain tub.

The relief washed over the nanny's face, and she stepped to the side so that Addison and Reed could rush in. Emily was sleeping. Thank God. And she was too little to remember the nightmare that'd just gone on around her.

Addison scooped the baby into her arms and pressed a flurry of kisses on her face. That woke Emily and the baby made a whining sound of protest, looking pretty sour as her gaze went from Addison to Reed.

He'd take a sour look over injuries any day.

Reed gave Emily some kisses as well, and probably because the nanny knew this would be a tearful reunion, she stepped out into the hall.

And the tears came all right. Several of them streaked down Addison's cheek.

"You said *Emily's parents,*" she pointed out.

It took Reed a moment to realize what she meant, but that was indeed what he'd said to the nanny so that she would know it was friend, not foe.

"Did you mean it?" she asked.

Reed was certain he gave Addison a funny look. "Of course." But the full impact of it hit him then.

They were Emily's parents.

Yes, Addison had gone through with the surrogacy without his knowledge or consent, but that no longer mattered. All that mattered was the beautiful little girl Addison was holding in her arms.

Well, maybe not all.

There was something else, too.

Reed leaned in and kissed first Emily on the cheek, and then he gave Addison a kiss on her mouth. One to let her know how relieved he was that she was all right. However, the attraction kicked in pretty darn fast, and he kissed her again just because that was what he wanted to do.

"Everything okay?" someone asked.

Because his nerves were still right there at the surface, Reed reeled around, bracing himself for more danger, but it was just Cooper making his way to them.

"We're fine," Reed answered, "but I still want Addison to see the doctor. Dominic's man shot her with a tranquilizer dart."

"The ambulance is on the way to check everybody out. Plus, we've got a couple of injuries."

"Any of them our men?" Reed asked quickly.

"No. All Dominic's triggermen." Cooper studied them again. "You're sure you're okay?"

Reed nodded, but whether or not that was true depended on what he learned from Cooper. "Did you round up all of Dominic's men?"

"Yes. The two here are spilling all because they're hoping for a plea deal now that their boss is dead and can no longer protect them."

"The one in the barn wants a plea deal, too, and he's offered to lead us to Dominic's files," Reed told him.

Cooper's face lit up. "Even better. I want all the loose ends tied up on these baby farms, and I'll cut a deal with the one who can make that happen the fastest."

Reed wanted the same thing, and even though it might take months to make that happen, it would be his top priority.

Right after Addison and Emily.

"I need some personal time off," Reed said to Cooper.

Cooper glanced at Addison and Emily, then smiled. "If you hadn't asked, I would have insisted you take it. Not a day or two, either. Make it at least two weeks. It's obvious you've got some loose ends of your own to deal with."

Yeah, and Reed could take care of one of those right now—to tell Addison that he was still in love with her and that he wanted both Emily and her in his life.

"I'm not going anywhere," Addison said before Reed

could speak. She winced, shook her head. "I mean, I'm not leaving Sweetwater Springs. Or you."

That last part really pleased Reed.

"Good. Because I had no intention of letting either one of you leave."

Addison gave him a smile, but it quickly vanished. "Is that because you feel obligated to take care of Emily?"

He was certain he frowned, and then Reed set her straight right off. He kissed the living daylights out of her and kept on kissing her until she sort of melted against him. The only reason he stopped the kiss was that Emily kicked him in the chest.

Reed laughed. And figured there'd be a lot more kicks, kisses and laughter in his future. Well, there would be if he got his way on this.

"Will you marry me…again?" he asked Addison.

She sucked in her breath so fast that she coughed. Obviously, he'd surprised her, though he didn't know why.

"You know I love you," he clarified. "Always have. Always will. There's no one else I'd ever want to marry. The thing is I only want to do it one more time, and then that's it. The final deal. No more loose ends, because I want Emily and you in my life forever."

And he waited. And waited.

But Addison just stood there staring at him.

Heck. He hadn't gotten this all wrong. He could see the love in her eyes. Could feel it in her kiss. Knew it was there, deep in her heart.

"Well?" he prompted.

Addison launched herself into his arms, getting as close to him as she possibly could, considering that she was still holding Emily.

"Pinch me, because I can't believe this is for real," Addison said, her breath all soft and silky.

"I'd rather kiss you than pinch you." And Reed started to do just that. Then he stopped. "But first, I'd like an answer to my marriage proposal."

"Yes," she blurted out.

Making him a very happy man indeed.

However, he held off on that kiss because he needed just one thing more. "Are you marrying me again out of obligation?" he asked.

A slow smile bent her mouth. "No. Because I love you. And because I want you in bed every night."

Yeah, definitely all the loose ends were gone. So Reed eased Addison to him and gave her that kiss.

* * * * *

Look for more books in USA TODAY *bestselling author Delores Fossen's miniseries,*
SWEETWATER RANCH, *later in 2015.*
You'll find them wherever
Harlequin Intrigue books are sold!

Bo McBride, accused but never arrested for the murder of his girlfriend two years ago, has finally returned to Lost Lagoon, Mississippi, to clear his name with Claire Silber's help. But it doesn't take long for them to realize that real danger stalks Claire.

Read on for a sneak preview of SCENE OF THE CRIME: KILLER COVE, the latest crime scene book from New York Times *bestselling author* Carla Cassidy.

"So, your turn. Tell me what you've been doing for the last two years," Claire asked. "Have you made yourself a new, happy life? Found a new love? I heard through the grapevine that you're living in Jackson now."

Bo nodded at the same time the sound of rain splattered against the window. "I opened a little bar and grill, Bo's Place, although it's nothing like the original." His dark brows tugged together in a frown, as if remembering the highly successful business he'd had here in town before he was ostracized.

He took another big drink and then continued, "There's no new woman in my life. I don't even have friends. Hell, I'm not even sure what I'm doing here with you."

"You're here because I'm a bossy woman," she replied. She got up to refill his glass. "And I thought you could use an extra friend while you're here."

She handed him the fresh drink and then curled back up

in the corner of the sofa. The rain fell steadily now. She turned on the end table lamp as the room darkened with the storm.

For a few minutes they remained silent. She could tell by his distant stare toward the opposite wall that he was lost inside his head.

Despite his somber expression, she couldn't help but feel a physical attraction to him that she'd never felt before. Still, that wasn't what had driven her to seek contact with him, to invite him into her home. She had an ulterior motive.

A low rumble of thunder seemed to pull him out of his head. He focused on her and offered a small smile of apology. "Sorry about that. I got lost in thoughts of everything I need to get done before I leave town."

"I wanted to talk to you about that," she said.

He raised a dark brow. "About all the things I need to take care of?"

"No, about you leaving town."

"What about it?"

She drew a deep breath, knowing she was putting her nose in business that wasn't her own, and yet unable to stop herself. "Doesn't it bother you knowing that Shelly's murderer is still walking these streets, free as a bird?"

His eyes narrowed slightly. "Why are you so sure I'm innocent?" he asked.

HIEXP0415